THE

MW01274593

Stories
by
Will Clattenburg

UnCollected Press

The Art of Fugue
Copyright © 2020 Will Clattenburg

Book Design by UnCollected Press
Cover Art: Will Clattenburg

UnCollected Press
8320 Main Street, 2nd Floor
Ellicott City, MD 21043

For more books by UnCollected Press:
www.therawartreview.com

First Edition 2020
ISBN: 978-1-71684-554-3

In memory of Tim Delehaunty, teacher

Table of Contents

Parallel Lines

Long after his wife had braised a whole chicken and called
him to dinner and they had made love on the kitchen
counter and he'd impregnated her and then watched with
the cautious fascination of a new parent as she'd grown taut
as an apple, her belly holding a porpoising life that
deepened her blue eyes and weighted her gestures, after
he'd commuted on the D train into and out of Manhattan
and he'd had the need for a pre-tax Metro-Card, he
remembered the girl who'd fastened her eyes on him after
the train, emerging from the station at 36th Street, clicked to
a stop on the tracks not yet within view of the vine-covered
fence across from the platform at his destination; the girl in a
blue peacoat that had been fashionable in New England
while he was an undergraduate, her hair in a careless braid,
voluminous and glossy, parting over her winter-warmed ears,
who had been eyeing him from halfway down the car as if
she'd known him from somewhere, not with confidence so
much as recognition, telegraphing to him her need for more
time, time for them to edge closer together, to close the
distance in the crowded train—and he'd stepped out at 9th
Avenue and watched from the platform as the car and her
framed face retreated, and the cool air of December felt
welcome as he walked home... his shadow had stayed on the
train, the imaginative part of him that he couldn't yet control,
and in that time and place, absolved of all responsibility (or
so he thought), he approached her and learned her name

1

was Dierdre—she worked in the city, she'd graduated from Brown, she lived in a refurbished house in Bensonhurst where it smelled like the ocean and seagulls scared away the pigeons and in summer a bougainvillea burst into tissue-paper blossoms on a white wicker fence on the path that led to the back of the house where she had a key—her bedroom just off the kitchen, a room barely big enough for a twin bed, but with high enough ceilings so she could raise her bed from the floor to make more room, a white desk in the corner, a mason jar with a fake sunflower, corkboard covered in scutes of overlapping pictures—and when he was with her, he understood that she was like him; she was from New England, like him, and had gone to school in the same environment where young people wore peacoats and plaid scarves, and no one admitted to any prejudice or questioned their own merits; she was well-off, she worked for a bank; she'd survived the implosion of 2008; she was no longer on the lowest rung; her New Year's bonus was so absurd she couldn't speak about it without feeling ashamed, especially when she found out what he made; she'd taken the same undergraduate classes as he had only with different professors who'd given their classes different names and she'd read the same books; she'd studied the same foreign languages and made the same decision not to travel abroad; in college, she'd lived in the same unisex style of dormitory; she'd dated people she cohabitated with; she'd learned to drink coffee only after college had ended, and —like him— still had a provincial wonder of New York (and that would never go away); she longed to make a decisive move but had always pulled back at the last minute out of an innate conservatism disguised as rational thought... and all these elements of her life had been present the day he saw her on the D train heading home... and her attempt to get his attention (she laughed as they lay on her little bed) was the boldest thing she'd done in a long time; it was an act of vulnerable exposure, not counting her ability to work and

2

talk under pressure which she considered more of a practiced ability, and she was so happy because her attempt had brought them together; they were happy together, a happy couple whom no one would question or complain about, except for him, later, holding his son, born to a woman totally unlike the girl on the train, grasping the solid, vulnerable, sleeping infant in a dark one-bedroom apartment and revolving in his mind how best to appease his imagination since now, as a father, his best creation was already done, and his imagination—only capable of shadows—kept carrying him down paths where he had never gone.

The Wedding

A few years ago, Colin took Rachel to the wedding of his
first college girlfriend, Juliet Levin. The wedding took place
outside Boston and the ceremony was very nice, but there
was one thing that irritated him: when the maid of honor
gave her speech about Juliet and how she had met her
husband Raymond (Ray) Lin in college, she didn't mention
Colin in connection with Juliet, even indirectly as in "Juliet
had a few boyfriends before she met Ray, but Ray was the
one, you could tell right away." Instead, the maid of honor
said that Juliet met Ray at the beginning of college and fell in
love with him, and that was that—they had some tests to their
relationship and whatnot but they held intact all four years. It
was as though the maid of honor, Kristin Chen, had excised
Colin from the history of Juliet's life. Which was not entirely
accurate. Colin and Juliet had dated the fall of their
freshman year—in many respects, they had developed
together during that impressionable time. Actually, Juliet had
gone through as many as four phases of personality and
career-orientation, which is normal for young people who
are still malleable and learning what is most essential to
know about themselves. When they first started dating, Juliet
was religious, almost devout. She was technically
Presbyterian, but she didn't know much about it. Instead she
went to a "high church" style Episcopal church where you
had to genuflect. She liked it so much she stayed for the
social hour right after the service and made friends with a

4

few young men who behaved and dressed like missionaries. By sophomore year, she discovered she was agnostic and officially switched her major from English to Biology. Before that, Juliet had wanted to major in English and gave every indication of becoming an English professor, one who would wear loose-fitting, autumnal-colored clothes with clashing floral and animal-skin prints. This particular phase—the phase of being interested in Chaucer and Beowulf and Montaigne's essays—lasted only one semester. By spring, Juliet was already doubling up on science classes and keeping meticulous color-coded notecards with lithographic renderings of organic and inorganic compounds; she memorized every card. A third phase involved championing women's rights through small scale activism including protests and marches which Colin still occasionally learned about since Juliet included him in her email chains even after they broke up. They were still friends throughout college—they just didn't speak for the five months after their breakup. In those five months, Juliet hooked up with a pothead named Orion and yearned to go on a road trip through South America. Her last phase of college was a sudden interest in the sports Ray played. On fall afternoons, she could be seen tossing a baseball or softball or frisbee on the quad. At 7 or 8 o'clock, she could be seen heading to the gym with Ray and his dormmates for a game of basketball. After they graduated, she studied to be a psychiatrist, and Colin was certain she went through even more phases, one of which was penning long emails to him about the need for "balance" and "mental health" vis-à-vis a significant other. Nevertheless at the wedding, Colin was left out of Juliet's life, though it was perfectly understandable that no one would mention the names of Juliet's and Ray's ex-boyfriends and ex-girlfriends at the celebration of their nuptials. But afterward, Colin was disoriented and (unusually for him) depressed. He shook hands with Ray. Juliet complimented Rachel on her dress. When they got back to their hotel, it

5

wasn't late. Colin drank a Sprite in a glass with ice and watched the movie *Memento* on TV with commercial breaks while Rachel read a paperback she'd bought at Penn Station, and he fell asleep with the dull sense that he'd accomplished a task.

Turnabout

If it wasn't depression in the clinical sense, it was close. All her days, all her hours. Here she was, just graduated from college, living at home. A prestigious college that her grandparents paid for, and no real job afterward. Every morning, she drove the forty-five minutes to Emmaus, New Jersey. Radio personalities talked in between songs for somebody else, a soundtrack for a life she'd outgrown. The grass along the highway was green, the color of magic markers. She parked at an office building with blue-tinted windows, took the elevator to the seventh floor, and found her supervisor each morning at five minutes to 9:00. The tests were already stacked in a small metal bin labeled TEMP on her supervisor's desk, about four or five standardized tests sealed with red, orange, and yellow stickers on which bold text read: Do Not Break the Seal, and which when opened released a mild floral odor from the soybean-based ink that came off on her hands like pollen. She carried the tests back to her desk in a generic cubicle that she shared with no one and then sat and read them, read the directions that never varied, the questions with five answer choices, matched what she read with the diagrams and visual accompaniments, the rather crude stick figures whose purpose was to demonstrate relative velocity or forensic science. It didn't matter if she understood the content—what mattered was grammatical correctness, that everything made logical sense. After the temp agency processed their fee, she received $11/hour. So she read tests. Her eyes sometimes hurt but they weren't cruel taskmasters. She could take breaks, have a coffee, gaze out the window at the field that horseshoed the parking lot. At 5:00 p.m., she handed her supervisor both her opened and unopened tests and drove in true rush hour back to her parents' house in Flourtown, Pennsylvania. Day after day, week after week. And then one day, she decided she didn't want to sit and read tests anymore. She called the temp agency and spoke with a nice woman named Angela who urged her to reconsider her decision—if she quit midweek, without giving two weeks' notice, the agency would have no choice but to terminate her contract; she would no longer be able to apply for future assignments! But she said *That's OK, thank you for everything* and hung up before Angela could give her more valid reasons for staying on the job. It was Wednesday, the month was July. She drove on I-95 South. Starting out, the sky was the color of sediment in a river. She approached Wilmington, Delaware on a stretch of blanched roadway, passing the brick buildings and factories. In a short while, she was in Maryland where deciduous trees, Virginia creeper, honeysuckle, redbuds, sumac, and forsythia curtained off and almost touched the road. Two hours later, she crossed the Potomac. The rain had held off until then, and now it looked like a faraway stippling against the surface of the Potomac where the river turned. Then, without warning, sheets of water began to hit her windshield. Still she drove, slower, following the other cars' brake lights, her car cutting through the crystal-like opacity of rain. The rain stopped, then resumed, then became very bad, her windshield wipers only capable of glazing her view, leaves and twigs striking the sides of the vehicle, getting wattled on the hubcaps and undercarriage. The car crunched and absorbed slaps and gentle swipes as it crushed along, spraying water and sliding in water and breaking water into a thousand droplets. There was never any danger of flooding;

8

the car was heavy, stately, a safe car for a safe girl who had always made safe decisions, a car her parents had bought her with safety in mind. So she observed the culverts and runoff and the new grass from the safety of her car, still pelted with rain. She hadn't checked her phone. It was going on noon. The storm had slowed her down. When it let up, she was driving through hills and copses of trees, dark foliage in the axillae of the landscape, everything washed and blurred, except at a distance she saw a heap of garbage bags. She slowed, then slowed even more. What looked like garbage bags was in fact a dead cow on the side of the road, legs spread as far as the rumble strips. In the light of recent rain, the cow was copper colored, darker the closer she got. She didn't stop. Even then it didn't look real. But the incident was filled with a gravitas that seeded itself in her mind. She didn't feel like she was in a hurry to understand its meaning. And for the next part of the drive, she was lighter, she could have laughed. She was not someone to make spur-of-the-moment decisions. She had been expecting something different, some uneasiness to work on her and reshape her mind, an uneasiness that would give her a new perspective on herself, a culminating answer to questions about her future. But the future comes slower than she'd anticipated. It would be future when the world was dry and all the leaves fell off her car and the grass in the gullies could breathe. She was not stopping. Be brave, she thought, be brave. She was entering a new phase of her life. The bloated cow had vanished from her rearview mirror. Ahead the road shone like obsidian.

Talking My Generation Blues

Madison was the girl who got me to quit listening to Led Zeppelin. I'm not sure why I put so much stock in her opinion—I guess I just wanted to get with her. Anyways, relationships are all about compromise, isn't that right? Give and take. *I'll curb this annoying habit if you curb that.* That kind of thing. I'm still not sure why she was especially offended by Led Zeppelin though. Maybe it was Robert Plant's voice. I can get that. I still remember all my liberal arts professors swooning over Leadbelly like he was at the vanguard of 20th century music, and I'd always thought if I had to listen to him everyday for the rest of my life I'd go insane—not to mention the poor woman who had to wake up every morning next to that face. As if the cheerful subject matter of his songs wasn't enough. Oh well. No accounting for taste. I was saying Led Zeppelin—Maggie said they were too "acid rock." She was speaking about *Houses of the Holy* since that was the only CD I routinely played back then. I'd listened to *Led Zeppelin IV* all through high school to the point where I'd scratched and damaged the original CD and, in the process, even after I bought a replacement, I'd lost interest. I couldn't listen to it anymore; I'd had enough. So I decided losing *Houses of the Holy* wasn't that big a deal either, as far as concessions went. Maybe Madison was doing me a favor, helping me outgrow some vestige of my boyhood or something. Like maybe adult men are supposed to outgrow Led Zeppelin the same way I'd outgrown Pearl Jam,

Ernest Hemingway's novels, Burger King, Big League Chew, Fruit by the Foot, and video games. Sure, not everyone outgrows video games, but by age eighteen or nineteen, I couldn't get into them anymore. I just wasn't interested enough. And so I theorized that everything peaks in your life, all your hobbies and enjoyments, and sometimes the peak is more like a plateau so it becomes a lifelong interest and other times the peak is sharp and jagged and afterwards your interest just dips and bottoms out. I didn't listen to *Houses of the Holy* and I even erased all my Led Zeppelin albums from my computer—this from back in the day when we burned CDs onto computers and made do with scuffs on the original CD. I didn't miss those albums the first few years we were together. I never one time had any regrets like *Gee, everything's swell, only I wish Madison hadn't outlawed me listening to Led Zeppelin.* And "outlaw" is really an exaggeration—all she did was criticize *Houses of the Holy* at face value when she heard it playing in the background. She'd just said, "What is this... acid rock? Psychedelia?" The thing is, I hadn't really considered Led Zeppelin to be acid rock at all—and I was on the point of explaining how I'd classify the band as more of blues rock, but I didn't. I didn't think it was worth the time or effort to explain. Besides, I'd been itching to get with Madison since we'd graduated college and ended up in the big city. Yeah, she'd known I was crazy about her and had been for years—waiting out her doomed relationship with this arrogant soccer-playing upperclassman, biding my time but always on friendly terms with her without any weird romantic overtures or bashful come-ons. I was pretty much upfront about how I felt and I left it at that. Otherwise, I was just someone to lend an ear and I don't know, I'm assuming she appreciated it since we remained friends all during college. Then, when we graduated and moved, that's when our relationship started. We were always hanging out, to the extent that I'd often have to cancel plans with people from work and with my roommates so I could see her. But I didn't mind, seeing her was much better. And we had all of New York for the beginning of our relationship. It was like the city existed in all its complex, impersonal busyness just as a backdrop for our free-spirited life. The dad of one of my exes used to tell me, "Live in New York when you're young. It's the best place for a young person to be." That dad, bless his heart, I'd pray every night to have him as a father-in-law, but it didn't work out—not that it should have. I was sixteen at the time, barely with a driver's license, and his daughter was the first girl who ever let me take off her bra. I learned a lot about bras from her in fact; for that, I will be forever grateful, though clumsiness at taking off bras is another mark of youth. When you get to your late twenties, in my experience, women just take off their own bras. Anyways, Madison never waited for me to take off her bra, except one time after a romantic dinner, but then on Valentine's Day or anniversaries, you pull out all the stops. Anyhow, the point of all that was that Madison and I were together and we were happy—we were a good team—and I put up with her Björk and Radiohead even though it struck me that *Houses of the Holy* wasn't much more psychedelic than some of what she listened to. Then after further conversation I learned that a major part of why she'd criticized *Houses of the Holy* on a general level was she believed that people of a given generation should listen to and appreciate the artists, writers, painters, etc. of their own generation, like somehow that was the appropriate thing to do—and if I needed more convincing just consider all the artists, writers, painters, etc. who hadn't received any appreciation at all from their contemporaries, only to be applauded later on as the geniuses they were. I was going to deconstruct her argument by the very fact that it was later generations who appreciated the ones who came earlier, but she must have anticipated my critique because she said that her standards of appreciation didn't apply to bands like Led Zeppelin or The Rolling

Stones since they were appreciated right away by their own generation—and in the end what I took from her argument was that artists deserved a certain quota of appreciation and once that quota was reached (the early 1970s in the case of Led Zeppelin) it was incumbent upon the next generation to find their own artists on whom to exhaust their appreciation until their own quota was met and so on and so forth. I couldn't quite get behind her logic 100%, especially when it came to writers and painters and sculptors, but I supposed it was an easier argument to make with regard to musicians. I would have brought up Destiny's Child or some group like that and asked her if you'd really want to listen to that brilliance all day instead of Martha Reeves or Carole King, but I didn't want to belittle her argument with the most outrageous comparisons I could think of. Besides, I knew what she meant had nothing to do with Destiny's Child—for her there would be much better examples of musicians who actually wrote their own songs in the 1990s and early 2000s, bands I'd never heard of or cared to know like Veruca Salt and The Raincoats and The Meat Puppets who are obvious examples of groups no one will appreciate in ten, twenty, or one hundred years except for the hardcore punk fanbase of Kurt Cobain. And the sad truth is even Nirvana hasn't aged too well over the years, probably because they weren't around long enough to develop and give themselves more variety other than their one angry jangle that was so much better than anyone else for two-three years circa 1992. I could say the same for Soundgarden, only "Fell on Black Days" sounds better now than it ever did. But I can't listen to anything else they ever played. And Madison's moved on from the 1990s too. When we were first together, she liked to go to small clubs and venues and make discoveries, and I went with her, but I always thought it was silly to try so hard to be on the cutting edge. Of course, in the types of clubs and places where we hung out, Madison's friends would drop band names like they were the true banner bearers of music, the more obscure and uncommercial the better, though to me most of these punk, alt-rock, anti-folk, grunge acts sounded the same, like they hadn't even mastered the whole breadth of Rancid's sound or Nirvana's chord progressions which made them even more limited in scope and, consequently, even more forgettable. Afterwards, Madison would ask me if I liked the Cocteau Twins or Kiera Lynn Cain or Trespasser William or Seamonkey and I'd lie and go with one of the four and pray I could tell the difference and she'd take me so seriously I felt compelled to expand on my lie and develop it and I'd get myself caught in a myriad of nonsense observations and comparisons. From Madison's serious, sleepy face I couldn't tell if I was impressing her or embarrassing myself. That's pretty much how things went for a while. Finally, one afternoon, I told her I'd been meditating on this whole music issue for a while and I'd had a heartfelt debate within myself and, other than Santigold and The Brazilian Girls, I hadn't enjoyed a single concert I'd been to in the last year. I especially hated Seamonkey. I detested Brothers Past. Bilge Vomit made me want to punch the lead singer. I'd never liked Billy Corgan, and his Nordic doppelganger in Bilge Vomit was equally repulsive. I'd rather listen to Belinda Carlisle than inflectionless female vocalists who sounded like monks. And I wouldn't trade *Houses of the Holy* for any of them. Madison nodded. Her face was super serious. I think she must have expected my rebellion one of these days. I told her I didn't mind her listening to all that garbage, but I'd be trying out Led Zeppelin one last time, and I'd prefer if she kept her opinions to herself as I would from that time on. *Houses of the Holy* sounded better than ever. "The Song Remains the Same" was almost brand-new. I tried *Led Zeppelin III* and liked all the acoustic songs too. I even unearthed the overplayed *IV.* Just as good—especially "Going to California." I didn't feel like I'd wasted anything holding onto these albums and I liked the opportunity to rediscover them. I was happy, maybe I'd been right all along. If you're thinking Madison and I broke up after that, think again—well, you can see for yourself we're still together. She did take offense to my comparing the bass player of Bilge Vomit to Billy Corgan. She admitted later that she'd had an intense crush on the guy but I shouldn't worry—it would've never worked out.

Wallace Made Good

Wallace had a few artistic ventures going—in her head. First:
she wanted to buy or dig around her parents' junk drawer
for one of those Kodak or Fuji self-winding cameras and use
it to take pictures of the oversize parking lots of abandoned
Big K's, Basco Bests, I Got it at Gary's, Superfreshes, Giant
supermarkets, and other bankrupt chain retail and grocery
stores. She'd hit on the idea while driving past a big chain
retail store with a dismantled marquee. The letters K and S
were still visible in pasty yellow and a clump of milk thistle
grew through the concrete base of an old sodium lamp that
had formerly helped guide late-evening shoppers back to the
farthest reaches of the parking lot where there wasn't even a
convenient corral for shopping carts. She would take
hundreds of photographs from all angles—eroded asphalt,
faded parking lines, dismembered shopping carts, moribund
vegetation. Her working title, "Reclaimed Parking Lot," had
spun around her head for a time, but recently she was
leaning toward "Obsolescence." She'd get to it someday. For
now, she kept busy sketching on cocktail napkins and
placing bets with herself whether her companion of the
moment would even notice what she was drawing. Although
it was laughable if she put it into words, Wallace had a
consistent goal for all her blind dates and liaisons and that
was that one night she would find herself drinking with a
prominent Manhattan art collector or museum curator or,
better, a wealthy philanthropist and patron of the arts who

just happened to be driving by car through this picturesque stretch of western PA where Wallace had relocated three years ago when she decided to join the hospitality industry. The arts patron would be archangelic and totally desexualized; in her visions, he would arrive fortuitously at Wallace's usual bar where she would be drinking rum and cokes with whatever lackluster companion of the night; he would notice Wallace's casual sketches on bar napkins and would understand that these sketches were not some atypical habit she'd adopted to impress anyone but rather a constant impulse, the impulse of all conditionally artistic minds. Seeing such incipient talent and potential, the arts patron would there and then offer her something to the tune of $24,000 as a loan, mind you, so she could quit working as a hospitality specialist and focus instead on the realization of her artistic promise. "Reclaimed Parking Lots"/"Obsolescence" was just the beginning. She had much bigger plans. For example: she was going to make a series of drawings on nude women. The drawings would be panoramas of city life, drawn in fine-tipped black Sharpie (Wallace's media of choice), with quarter-inch, Keith Haring-inspired human silhouettes performing all life's daily functions: riding buses and trains, donning hard hats at construction sites, attending alternative schools, unloading patients from ambulances into hospitals, passing through airport security, buffing their nails at beauty salons, scarfing down plates of Pakistani-style samosas from small establishments on Crosby Street. However, the genius of the project was not even in the drawings—the genius was in the choice each viewer would have to make between staring at the intricate details of Wallace's drawings or staring inches away at breasts, buttocks and genitalia. The exhibition would create a fundamental crisis between these two desires, these two aesthetics—art or intimate body parts. The title was going to be "Façade." Wallace couldn't wait to explain it all. Only after the rich arts patron had joined Wallace for a second or third drink, which would double his appreciation of her giftedness, after the night had passed a certain point and there would be "no going back," no retraction, only then would Wallace reveal the knockout punch, a piece she knew would earn her worldwide renown: a piece called "The Hive." What was it? Nothing, except for a human-sized replica of an actual beehive, a skeleton of wooden ribs papered over with *Daily News* articles slathered in Mod Podge. Wallace got the idea from the famous exhibit "Flags," which she had gone to see while living in the hallway of her friend Isabel's apartment on the Bowery, a time in her life which she nostalgically referred to as "The Purge" for reasons that were not germane to the conversation she would be having with the avuncular, happily married arts patron who would never once stroke Wallace's hand or attempt to flirt. Her idea would never get old, either. She could do it today or ten years from now and it would achieve the same effect. She was almost happy to wait and keep the idea to herself. She was certainly happy whenever she pictured the crowds of people waiting to view "The Hive." The structure would be placed at the edge of the Sheep's Meadow near the restrooms. Visitors would form a curlicuing line by the fence where a single security guard, picking dogshit off the heel of his boots, would be yelling, "Only four at a time in 'The Hive.' Excuse me, wait your turn, bud. Only four at a time in 'The Hive.' Did you hear what I just said, pal?" Everyone would be jostling for their chance to walk inside and see why they'd stood in line for two hours. After they were inside, still jostling and jostled, now shoulder to shoulder with strangers in the tight air reeking of Mod Podge, Wallace bet she could just hear them say, "Well, this is art, isn't it? Shows what I know." This project gave her more satisfaction than all the others, and just about made life bearable.

Interlude

Shannon was the sexiest woman I've ever seen in slacks. I mean, lots of women can look sexy in slacks, but Shannon looked like she was made for slacks, like slacks did something for her body that maybe a dress couldn't even do, the way they fit her, just loose enough on her calves, but tight enough on her thighs, so that they flicked just a bit when she walked, but also hugged her butt. (And she did wear dresses, it wasn't like she didn't wear dresses or she only wore slacks. She didn't wear slacks on principal either, or because she was even aware of the overall sexy effect they had on casual male strangers like me—though I'd like to think I was more than a stranger since we knew each other peripherally, I mean, I was dating her roommate. There wasn't some grand design to her whole slacks-wearing preference but—if I had to offer an opinion—I wasn't a huge fan of the dresses she wore. It was like she wore her dresses out of spite or just because she owned them and didn't want to buy any others, like the way my high school girlfriend Louise used to wear these old white bras held together by safety pins, probably figuring she'd never be in a situation where those safety pins were an issue. So, like I was saying, Shannon would wear these old dresses over and over again until they lost their sheen, and developed honey-colored stains under the armpits, and more or less came to resemble the dismal dresses of forgotten mannequins, and it wasn't as if some dude she was dating could influence her otherwise, by

19

saying: "You know, I think you might want to buy a new dress" *hint hint*, since Shannon was an independent thinker and actually got in fist fights with people who suggested she change her behavior, even on simple things like cutting her toe nails, or wearing a more neutral blush.) Shannon's slacks were professional and sexy. She could have been an economics professor, or maybe a hotel liaison, or an actor playing a desk attendant in an insurance commercial, or perhaps a facilitator for a focus group; with slacks like that she could have been anything. I would have loved to be in a focus group with Shannon, but that's neither here nor there. (And, in fact, participating in a focus group is never as much "fun" as it's cracked up to be no matter who your facilitator is.)

Another thing about Shannon was she actively disliked men who gave her flowers. She wouldn't get in a fist fight with you if you happened to give her flowers or present her with a rose on Valentine's day, but she wouldn't talk to you for a week just to let you know the gesture wasn't appreciated and please God never do it again. Shannon's boyfriends never understood her flower aversion, and most men had no idea what went wrong when instead of being rewarded by kisses and romantic caresses, Shannon turned away from them in anger and appeared on the verge of tears or hysteria until, placing their hand on her shoulder the way we do when we're unsure whether or not we're even required, she'd look back, bite her lip, suck in her hair, blow out exasperatedly, and say, "Whew... Sorry... I just really... hate... flowers." While I may someday forget Shannon's slacks, and exactly what her face looked like, despite its amazing symmetry and the gray-green tincture of her eyes, usually shielded behind sunglasses when she glided along the street, or even how truly awful all her dresses were, I'll never forget her absolute hatred for receiving flowers. Even now, years afterward, I still have a hitch, like a knot in my stomach, a momentary hesitation, whenever I buy flowers,

20

and in fact, I once defended my wife Jill's brother from the charge of never buying his ex-fiancée flowers with the argument "maybe she was the type of girl who doesn't like flowers." Jill was like, "No girl doesn't like flowers." "That's not true," I said. I told her about Shannon. But Jill was like, "No girl doesn't like flowers. She was just saying that." And I was like, "No, I'm pretty sure she meant it." But Jill was like, "I've never met a girl who doesn't like flowers. She just said that, but she really meant she wanted them." "So, in other words, you're saying that instead of saying she wanted flowers, she said she hated when men gave her flowers, just so men would buy her flowers?" "Exactly." "Why not just say I want flowers?" "Don't you know anything about women?" "Are you saying, by saying 'I want flowers,' the interpretation is 'I don't want flowers'?" "I'm not saying anything. You're saying it." "So if you're saying 'I don't want flowers' actually means you do want flowers, would it also be true if you say, 'Get me flowers,' you really mean 'I don't want flowers'?" "No—and I'm not listening anymore. La la la di da." "So in other words, women always want flowers." "That's just what I've been telling you." "And I'm telling you that some women, rare exceptions they may be, do not want flowers." "Well, I want flowers and I'm the only woman you should be concerned about." "Well, but maybe your brother's ex-fiancée is the type of woman who really doesn't want flowers. Maybe flowers for some reason piss her off." "Ughhhhhhhhhhhh. You're impossible to deal with!" It turned out that Jill was correct at least in the case of her brother's ex-fiancée. When they were breaking up, in one of their bitter, cathartic, revelatory (too little too late) conversations, the ex-fiancée said, "And another thing. You never ever got me any fucking flowers!" To which Jill's brother was like, "But you *said* you never wanted them! {sob!}."

The Mannerists

I.

Despite her best efforts, Jessica Newsham was unable to make close friends in high school. In fact, during her second year, her attempts to become intimate with a group of girls culminated in the biggest embarrassment of her social life so far. What happened was this: Jessica had gone over to her friend Sybil's pool that summer because she knew some other girls would be there. She wasn't very good friends with Sybil, but she liked Sybil's friends Maggie and Neva, and she considered Fiona Yates (less frequently seen at Sybil's) to be the standard of what a high school friend should be although she never said so to Fiona or anyone else for that matter. Jessica had come into her new high school at a disadvantage, transferring to this elite college-preparatory high school her sophomore year after her family moved from Bucks County to Philadelphia. The high school her parents chose for her with only her nominal consent had a graduating class of 38 girls and 43 boys and what's more Jessica was one of only two new students that year—the other new student, a girl, was on athletic scholarship for track and field and quickly assimilated into the athletic clique who sat at the front table in the cafeteria and drank full glasses of chocolate milk. All the girls in Jessica's class knew each other on an encyclopedic level. Some of them had attended the elementary branch of this same high school and were what were called "lifers" at the school. There were fifteen core "lifers" in Jessica's class. Which wasn't to say that all the lifers were "cool" or on the "in crowd" or even the type of girls Jessica would choose to hang out with. But Maggie and Neva and Fiona were. They were all such good friends along with a few others including Sybil who wasn't a "lifer" but had transferred way earlier than Jessica—in 8th grade to be exact—and had ingratiated herself with all her classmates on account of the pool in her backyard and her notorious summer parties. Sybil's parents traveled often; they had a somewhat lax view of parenthood; they gave Sybil and her big sister Candace a lot of freedom "to be girls," way more freedom than Jessica and her sister ever enjoyed. Jessica was a bit intoxicated with this freedom.

That summer, she lay out with Maggie and Neva and Sybil in Sybil's expansive backyard and the girls smoked cigarettes and drank vodka mixed with tropical juices and for none of the girls was this out of the ordinary or even something worth commenting about. It just happened. School was over and done with. They didn't work in the afternoons, and Sybil and Neva didn't work at all. Come to think of it, the only one who really worked a full-time summer job was Fiona. That's why she wasn't there most times. Jessica's dad didn't think it necessary or important for Jessica to work in the summer. He was kind of aloof as far as dads went. His main belief was in Jessica's education. He read her report card every semester and then grilled Jessica on the subjects where she had received low grades, like she'd intentionally withheld her best effort. As was typical in families with two siblings, Jessica's dad never grilled Jessica's younger sister Kate at all and gave Kate the type of leeway that Jessica would have begged for, and even when Kate got all C's their dad didn't care or show any outward signs of perturbance. It was all on Jessica to make him proud. Kate was the baby of the family and was already quite good looking. She was the type of younger daughter who had

23

transcended the good looks of both her parents and become an exotic, renegade beauty with facial features like a new minted coin. Not that Jessica was bad looking. She was blonde and tall like her parents and not too chubby—it was only her face that bothered her. She had a roll under her chin and in general her face had stayed round and pudgy while her body had expanded and become womanly. She wasn't overweight per se, but she was thick in a voluptuous way, and she wore size C bras and was secretly vain about her breasts which she thought of as her best feature. So Jessica enjoyed going to Sybil's house so she could show off her body in her two-piece swimsuit that her mom hadn't really wanted to buy her, and she could feel pride in the fact that of the three girls she had the most developed body by far, not counting Fiona who really was like a full grown woman and even had a slightly damaged maybe gray tooth when she smiled that ironically enhanced her attractiveness and made it perfectly understandable when she showed up to some of Sybil's parties late with a college boyfriend quite a bit older than everybody else and distinguished by a receding hairline and salt and pepper sideburns and an out-and-out self-possession that made the high school boys feel inferior.

It was Fiona not even Sybil who first invited Jessica to Sybil's pool. As she herself would admit, Jessica wasn't really good friends with Sybil. Actually, the more Jessica went to Sybil's house, the more she understood that none of the girls were really "good friends" with Sybil in the sense of friendship as intimacy and good faith. Sure, they tolerated her and weren't ever mean; these were nice girls to begin with. They included Sybil in their groups, they invited her to the country club where Sybil wasn't a member (someone said that the country club didn't allow Jewish people to become members but Jessica couldn't believe that—or maybe she felt too ashamed to believe it). They invited Sybil to the mall, to the nail salon, to lunch, to boys' houses and parties with or without the boys' permission. Yet even though Sybil was always around, the others held something back from her. It was like they were sharing only one side of themselves, like the gear or mechanism that allows everyone to shift between many personalities had become locked in place, creating a sort of artificial, stilted formality between them. It seemed Sybil had access to only so much of their lives—the crucial, most important parts of themselves they compartmentalized and locked away when they were around her. Jessica understood how the girls were with Sybil because truth be told they were the same with her. But she was still the new girl, they didn't know her as well, so Jessica could better understand why they hadn't fully incorporated her into their group. Sybil, on the other hand, expected her friends to reciprocate after she invited them over. When invitations didn't come Sybil would call Neva and Maggie and even Fiona to try to invite herself. Jessica was in Maggie's kitchen one afternoon when Sybil called for exactly this purpose. The phone rang and Maggie went "Hello." Then: "Hi Sybil. No. Not much. I'm not feeling up for laying out. No—no one's with me." Maggie grinned at Jessica and Neva. "How 'bout tomorrow? OK. Tomorrow then. Bye Sybs." Then Maggie hung up and they left it at that.

Another time Sybil called and Neva (who was the closest to being mean out of all of them) went, "If it's Sybil, tell her '*abstinence* makes the heart grow fonder.'" The girls snickered, but Jessica was uneasy. She was reminded of how lonely she felt, learning to like these girls at her new school. She didn't particularly like Sybil, and she had a fun time without her, but it hurt to hear the girls talk about avoiding Sybil behind her back. She wondered if they said similar things about her. Still—she enjoyed being around the other girls too much to think of herself as just a follower, someone they were obliged to put up with because they were, for the most part, genuinely nice girls.

II.

Over June and into July, Sybil started calling Jessica. The first time she called, Jessica was out with Maggie and Neva and their boyfriends and she had come home breathless and excited because the boyfriends, Alex and Daniel, had said they'd wanted to set Jessica up with Roger Lusch. They were at the country club tanning and Alex and Daniel held Maggie's and Neva's hands and stroked them and Alex tickled Maggie until she warned him she was going to pee herself and then she'd changed positions so that her bikini line was visible and adjusted her swimsuit so the fabric was only an inch away from her crotch lying with her eyes closed and her entire body more or less on display without a care in the world.

Jessica's sister Kate told Jessica she'd had a call. Kate was into being dramatic and she knew Jessica hadn't made many friends. Jessica rolled her eyes and asked who it was. Kate told her it was Sybil Kaufman. She pronounced her name "Syb-bell."

Sybil had left her number and everything which was unnecessary because their phone had caller ID. Jessica didn't call her back just then. She took off her swimsuit and relaxed in the shower and thought about Alex and Daniel and their hands all over Maggie and Neva. She knew Maggie and Neva had sex with them and Maggie gave Alex blowjobs and she said her nipples got hard when she saw him without his shirt on and she talked about his penis like it was vanilla ice cream, something she just had to have, how it responded with just one stroke, so big, filling her up. Neva was much more discreet, but she and Daniel had sex too, Jessica thought. At the pool, Neva whispered to Daniel while they sat side by side. Jessica didn't listen to them whisper, but sometimes Neva's voice caught like she had a lump in her throat, and Jessica heard or thought she heard Neva asking Daniel to wait—that it would happen—later—but wait. Neva

26

was so sarcastic and she had such a hard edge with the girls, but with Daniel she was tender and gentle, like they had been married already and she was showing her personality as a wife. While Jessica showered she decided if she had a regular boyfriend she would behave like Neva. But Daniel was also different than Alex. He was less cocky, he didn't seem so sure of himself. He had dark hair and light eyes which Jessica hadn't determined if they were hazel or green/gray. She liked that she'd kept the color of his eyes vague. It meant someday she would notice the exact color of his eyes and all this pleasant vagueness—part of the feeling she was having this very moment—would disappear into a bittersweet reality. It was all hypothetical but as she took a shower in her bathroom after getting back, she decided that her true personality was more like Neva's anyway: she was gentle and discreet, she wouldn't want to broadcast her doings to her friends. If Daniel were her boyfriend she would act exactly as Neva acted. Anything else would be exaggerated. She wrung out her hair and tied her towel into a turban around her wet hair then went to return Sybil's call. Their conversation wasn't very long, but Jessica thought Sybil sounded disappointed; maybe she'd also been drinking. Jessica wondered who with.

"Do you feel like laying out tomorrow?" Sybil asked. "It would just be me and you. Neva's going to the shore and Maggie has to watch her brother. Fiona's... well. Fiona's too good for us."

Jessica didn't answer right away—long enough for there to be a silence. She had wanted so much to be friends with Maggie and Neva and Fiona. That's what she thought was happening this summer. That was why she put up with Maggie's promiscuity and Neva's sour attitude. But when it came down to it, she was in the same position as Sybil, left out and uninformed. She had been at the pool all morning with Maggie and Neva and neither one of them had shared

27

their plans for the next day with her. True, they'd talked about setting her up but they hadn't made any definite plans: were they even serious about Roger Lusch liking her? And was she even convinced that she could like him? The fluttery, nervous feeling that Jessica had carried in her belly since she returned home suddenly flattened out—and she felt the same hollow sadness she'd felt when Sybil called Maggie at her home and Maggie had laughed about it. Now Sybil was calling her, now Jessica was the one Sybil was trying to reach. Sybil was taking what she could get, she was starting to understand how her friendships really stood.

"Sure," Jessica said. "What time were you thinking?"

"Around nine o'clock?"

Jessica nodded and said "Sure" at the same time.

"Nine then."

Jessica's gentle, easy-going personality was good not just for boys but for friends of friends as well.

III.

Sybil's pool was small and kidney shaped with one set of stairs and a railing. Its deepest was six feet. The pool was separated from the house by a large rectangular patio paved with pinkish-gray flagstones. There were flowerbeds along the house and patio, and the gardens were professionally maintained by landscapers who came every Saturday—the grass was plush and dense and the dead flowers had been culled from the daylilies and geraniums and irises along the stone wall of the house. Behind the pool there was a magnolia tree, no longer in bloom, and a knobby linden that provided shade on the deeper end of the pool and along the concrete pool deck where the girls went when it got too hot.

When Jessica arrived, Sybil had arranged two pool chairs side by side in complete sun. She wore a white bikini and was using tanning oil. Her skin was already dark, darker than the other girls', and her light brown hair had streaks of blonde that she claimed were only a result of sun.

"Do you want a cigarette?" Sybil asked.

Jessica shook her head.

"Drink?"

Sybil went to fetch her a drink anyway—something pink in a tall glass that looked very thin and breakable. Jessica sat on the pool chair without a towel and sipped her drink slowly. All she could taste was grapefruit juice. The girls were alone just like Jessica had predicted. She had taken Sybil at her word about Maggie and Neva having other plans. She'd almost called Fiona but then decided not to at the last minute. She didn't want Fiona to know she was planning to go to Sybil's without her. Fiona was the most mature of all her classmates. Probably she wouldn't care if Jessica developed a friendship with Sybil. But Jessica didn't want anyone else to know she was hanging out alone with her, especially not Maggie and Neva. What she didn't want was for them to think of *her* as another Sybil—an unnecessary and even burdensome friend who try as she might could never win their complete friendship or trust. Being with Sybil only made her feel like more of an outsider—it seemed hopeless to even think she would be on a better footing with Maggie and Neva now. After taking a few forced sips of her drink, Jessica started to mellow. "I'm not much a drinker," she said.

Sybil was lying on her stomach. She had draped her bikini top over the end of her pool chair so she could brown her back. The tan line from her bikini was faint—caramel colored against the milk chocolate color of her back. Jessica didn't think she would ever tan so naturally. "I know it," Sybil said. "I've seen you when everyone's downing screwdrivers. I'm like wondering 'what does she think of us?' all sober when we're all drunk talking."

"When I drink too much," Jessica said, "I act stupid."

"I can't see you ever drinking too much."

Jessica didn't really mind if Sybil teased her. It was true she didn't drink too much. She actually didn't know how she would feel or what would happen if she did. The most she drank was a glass of brandy one New Year's when she was home with her sister Kate. Kate had put her up to it, and they'd both taken a few sips, then Kate dared her to drink a glass. Jessica did. She almost vomited—not really from the taste, which was sweet, but from the charge it sent down her throat and through her body. She spent the next hour drinking water out of the same glass. Kate had felt bad afterward—she'd sat with Jessica and hugged her and they went to sleep laughing because whenever Jessica burped it smelled and tasted syrupy and rich like the smell of their parents after a late-night party with friends. Jessica didn't like the taste of most drinks anyway—not that she'd sampled many of them. Now she could already feel the effects of whatever small amount of alcohol was in her grapefruit drink. It was making her head swim around. But she didn't feel uncomfortable. Overheard there were locusts and the summer morning was pulsing, the sun white-hot in the sky. Jessica took off her shorts and T-shirt and lay on the pool chair. A fly landed on Sybil's leg. Jessica started to tell Sybil the story of when she drank brandy with her sister. Halfway through Sybil made a noise like she was stretching and Jessica wished she hadn't chose this story. She sounded lame to herself, highlighting her total inexperience and the fact that her younger sister was more of a daredevil than she was.

"I love it," Sybil said when she was done. "That's you in a nutshell. I hope you don't mind me saying this but sometimes I think you're from another country."

"But I'm not," Jessica said, aware that her drinking was making her talk in an odd plainspoken manner. "I'm from Pennsylvania."

"Is this how everyone is from your part of the state?"

"How do you mean?" Jessica said.

"Nevermind. I'm teasing. Please if you ever feel like I'm ragging on you just say 'Sybil, stop being a bitch.' I'll totally understand." Sybil got up and put on her bikini top. She had small, flat boobs and dark nipples that were larger than Jessica's but looked out of place on her small chest. "You're not angry with me?"

"No," Jessica said.

"Good. I'm getting you another drink. I've been so wanting to hang out with you. I'm glad you're here."

Jessica hadn't finished her first drink, or at least she thought she hadn't, but what she had finished had put a wobble to everything around her: the trees, the leaves skimming the surface of the pool, the lawn like a green sheet stretched to the far corner of the house. She took the glass from Sybil's hand and lay back down, surrendering herself to this new teetering dimensionality.

"You know what," Sybil said. "You must get a little sick and tired of hearing Maggie go on and on about Alex and his glorious dick. I do."

Jessica brushed a fly off her stomach.

"It's getting old," Sybil said. "Everyone thinks so."

"But no one says anything."

"I think I will next time. It's not like there isn't anything else to talk about in the world. It's like watching a TV tuned to the same channel, you know, the way it is with boys when all they talk about is football and basketball and barf. That's all right a little bit but not as an obsession. Does Maggie think she's the only girl who's ever done it?"

"It does get a little extreme," Jessica said.

"A little? Try *like* pornographic. I think she's trying too hard if you ask me. Alex isn't even all that cute. The hair. I mean, how does he get the front part to be curly like that? Plus have you ever actually talked to him for more than five minutes? It's like talking to a rock. I mean, I don't think he could maintain a conversation longer than two minutes. No wonder they're always doing it every chance they get.

Skip the small talk, straight to the action. I know, I know, I'm being unfair—I'm a spiteful bitch. Just tell me if I'm bothering you. Am I? Be honest."

"No," Jessica said. She had almost finished her second drink but she wasn't concentrating on it. "I agree with you." She was becoming careless now. "Daniel, on the other hand..."

Sybil shifted on her chair. "Daniel?"

"Nothing. Nevermind." Jessica set down her glass and felt a wave of nausea or the need to hiccup corkscrew up her throat and mouth. Her forehead was suddenly warm.

"Daniel," Sybil repeated. She was thoughtful. "You like him." This wasn't a question.

"I'm sorry. I told you I say stupid things when I drink."

"You don't have to apologize to me." Sybil paused as if she had something else to say. Then she went, "You never know how things turn out."

Jessica took another long drink, more or less finishing it, and this time her drinking was deliberate, like she needed to chase something down. "What do you mean 'how things turn out'?"

"Listen," Sybil said. She sat at the end of Jessica's pool chair, just perched at the end. Her position didn't look comfortable but she was a small person, barely five feet tall with thin hips and thin calves, thin every which way, especially compared to Jessica who looked like a lumbering giantess by comparison—so thick! "I'm going to be honest with you, one hundred percent honest. Not in some sick porno way like Maggie, I'm just going to tell you what I've noticed. Maggie, Neva, all of them. Watch out for them. It's something I've observed at this school—it's almost like a cult. They're two-faced. They smile and on the surface they're the nicest people ever, but then they'll talk about you behind your back, spread rumors. That's the kind of friends I can do without, thank you very much. Haven't you noticed?

You're a smart girl, Jessica. You see how they all come over here—chattering and happy. But God forbid I ever need one of them—really need somebody—then poof. They vanish." Sybil spread her hands imitating an explosion. "That's what I mean by two-faced. It's part of why I invited you to come over. I wanted to warn you. You're new so you don't know them like I do. Don't make the mistake of believing they're your friends. Another drink?"

"I really shouldn't," Jessica said. "I should get back."

"Don't be a lame-o. You can't drive now. Wait around, my sister's boyfriend will bring pizza—free, he gets it. What else do you have to do all day?"

So Jessica stayed. Sybil was right—she didn't have anything else to do.

IV.

After Sybil had established this connection with Jessica, it was always there. Whenever they were together, Jessica just had to look at Sybil to know her secret thoughts about their other friends. Sometimes Sybil would deliberately stare at her as if to say "I told you so!"

Jessica went to Sybil's house six or seven more times that summer, counting the last time—the party where the embarrassing incident happened. Sometimes Maggie and Neva and Fiona were there and sometimes not. Sybil didn't really communicate if the others were coming and Jessica, feeling pathetic and pitiful, didn't ask. She didn't want Sybil to think she was coming only for them—although that was really the reason she had started going in the first place. She was confused and was having a hard time making up her mind about Sybil. If what Sybil said was true, then Sybil really was her friend, and it would be good to have a friend she could trust. But if Sybil was lying, then her only purpose was driving Jessica away from the others, from Maggie and Neva and Fiona, the girls she had first wanted to be friends with—the girls that, to her, symbolized perfect friendship. But now, after hearing Sybil call them "two-faced," she asked herself what she really liked about them. What had been so appealing about them from the first? Was it their popularity? The fact that they seemed to exist at the epicenter of the class, with everyone else spinning around them, either pulled toward them like her or trying unsuccessfully to get away from them, like Sybil? To hear Sybil talk about them now, it was like the only reason she had invited the group to her house at all was so she could get closer to Jessica. It was Jessica who she really liked, but she hadn't been sure how deep Jessica was with the other girls. Then when she discovered that the other girls dropped Jessica just as casually as they'd dropped her, Sybil decided Jessica was OK—that was when she'd invited her over.

But Jessica wished she had never accepted the invitation. She wished she had never established this secret contact with Sybil apart from the other girls. And then on top of that she felt guilty about wanting to cut Sybil off. She just didn't click with Sybil, that was all. That was what Jessica decided finally and it was a satisfying enough conclusion. She liked Maggie and Neva and especially Fiona better than she liked Sybil. It had nothing to do with what they talked about or their tastes or what country club they belonged to; she was just more compatible with the others. Why had she gone to Sybil's? She felt hollow and disingenuous now with Sybil and with the others. A shift had occurred in her friendship, even the others noticed. Now Neva and Maggie never called to invite her over to Sybil's. Sybil called her herself. It made more sense, and it certainly was more polite for Jessica to accept an invitation from the person who actually lived at the house she was going to, but it marked a downslide in her relationship with Maggie and Neva. Maybe they knew how Sybil really felt about them. They knew that Sybil and Jessica talked about them. They sensed Jessica's betrayal and resented her. Or maybe Sybil had been right all along—they were the two-faced ones and in her eagerness to make friends Jessica had completely misread the situation. What made it worse was that Jessica had really betrayed them; she felt that way. She admitted to Sybil that she couldn't stand the way Maggie talked. Like a little kid she had complained about Neva's sarcasm and how Neva sometimes hurt her feelings. Sybil was sympathetic to all this. She seemed to like that they were becoming closer and closer.

"I have the insider's scoop on Neva," she said one day. They were by themselves, drinking, only the alcohol was slow to take effect on Jessica. She was proud of her new tolerance; it allowed her to keep up with Sybil but become cautious just in case the conversation went somewhere Jessica didn't want to go. "Did you know she's a virgin?"

"No way!" Jessica said.

"Not exactly a virgin. But she's only done it one time and not with Daniel. They do other things, but she won't let him go for it. She wants to wait for the right moment. Who knew she was so romantic?"

Jessica wasn't sure what to do with this new information. She was sure Sybil wanted to be hurtful, to disparage Neva. But Jessica couldn't help identifying even more with her other friend. She felt her own sensitivity pulling her back, putting her on guard, making her aware that she would never be quite like Sybil, no matter how many drinks she had.

"Daniel's losing patience."

Jessica sat up. She tuned out everything—all the summer noises—except Sybil's voice. "He's close to dumping her. Moving on. Greener pastures. Can't wait forever, you know. By the way, he's coming to my party this Saturday. It'll be all the usual suspects. Jeff Lieberson, Danny Bonaventura, Daniel Weatherby of course, Alex and his stoner friends, Roger Draft Dodger, Ian Hopson, Ron Plunkett, Will Vanderslice, Jana's little brother, plus my sister and her college friends. Fiona's a question mark.

35

Neva's definitely not coming—it's her shore week with her step-dad and their family. Don't know about Maggie, but if Alex *is* and there's a chance to have sex, I can't imagine her turning it down."

Jessica finished her drink for the small rush it gave. There had been no more discussion about setting her up with Roger Lusch. The last time she'd seen Maggie, she'd been grumpy because her parents were making her meet with a tutor to raise her math grade. It had been a cloudy day at the pool and Maggie's eyes had been red from crying.

"They told her she has to break up with Alex," Neva said. "They found weed in her bedroom. She says she put it in the drawer, so how could they know and it's like she can't even trust her parents to stay out of her room." That was the last any of them told her anything, and Neva didn't tell her like it was a secret. It was just matter-of-fact reporting. Fiona was leaving to go on a road trip with her boyfriend in August. When Jessica called, Fiona said she'd just taken mushrooms and was leaving in an hour to go to an art exhibit in New York City. Fiona only drank red wine now and said she was too old to hang out at the kiddie pool with Sybil and Maggie. She explicitly mentioned Sybil and Maggie, not Neva, as if she still had some respect for her. But Sybil and Maggie, strangely enough, always spoke about Fiona like she was their lifelong friend. She seemed to be the only one of them who wasn't "two-faced" in Sybil's opinion.

"Daniel's definitely coming?" Jessica said.

"Sure. We're good friends, you know." Sybil was confiding now. "I always talk to him and he calls me all the time when he wants someone to really listen. Most of the time, we talk about your epic crush on him."

"Come on!"

"I'm joking. But I'm sure he notices. I mean, he's sensitive, not a meathead or a stoner like Alex. He's too good for Neva."

"It's true I have a crush on him," Jessica said.

36

"Duh! You spilled the beans a while ago."

"You didn't tell anybody?"

Sybil must have thought she sounded worried. "No, I didn't," she said. "I'm not a gossip like your WASPy friends."

"They aren't my friends." Jessica didn't feel the impact of these words until afterward. And she didn't understand in the moment why she wanted to be so close to Sybil until a long time after, even after the event that would unravel much of her careful, risk-free life. "Not really. I don't know." She was flushed. The stubble under her arms stung. Her gross, oversized body started to sweat. She tried to change the subject. Sybil was staring at her. Her face was very thin and angular and pretty in a girlish way that the others had outgrown.

"What'd they do to you?" Sybil said. She didn't sound all too friendly now, but Jessica was looking and hearing her as if through gauze or some opaque, sound-muffling substance. When she talked she had the sensation of being underwater, her voice amplified, with an illusion of total privacy even as she could see, faintly, how her words were shaping Sybil's expression.

"Nothing. They just... forget about me like you said. I feel like they ignore me."

Sybil snorted. "Better to be ignored than betrayed," she said. She stood and walked back to the house, her bikini wedged between her bottom. It was such an abrupt departure Jessica felt like she had lost her voice, lost her ability to breathe.

V.

The night Jessica suffered her embarrassing revelation started in the usual way: preparations, staring at the mirror, fending off nervousness about decisions great and small. Jessica had already been to parties at Sybil's house, but this night was different. Even if she hadn't known that Neva wasn't going to be there—it was different—it had to do with her self-perception. Something like a wall or obstacle had come falling to the ground. On the other side of the wall was Daniel. Jessica was moving closer to him. But this was not the old Jessica with her insecurities; somehow, in the intervening days, she'd accepted her body, accepted the way she didn't tan but didn't redden either, accepted the new weight she'd inherited and the satisfying, mysterious pulse that seemed to run like a cord through her belly. Soon she would be face to face with Daniel in this new body that was totally hers. This was how she felt, like she'd grown into a new body, as she took a few moments to groom herself and notice her shape and figure. For so long she'd thought of her body as gross and oversized, but not anymore. She had just become a woman faster; she hadn't had time to adjust. She stood back, proud and delighted with her new heft. She had a new unashamed solidity. Maybe she had been this way for a while, but tonight she felt happy if still somewhat nervous with the way she looked. If boys at the pool wanted to set her up with other boys, that was only natural. But she wanted to choose for herself.

She wore a splash of her mother's perfume, but even the smell of perfume couldn't match the new sophistication she felt just by getting dressed, in putting on her underwear and bra and slipping into her size 8 black and white striped A-line dress she'd worn to formal and her wrap sandals which she'd aired out for a week to get rid of the smell of feet. On the way to Sybil's house, she kept the window down and the humid air worked to smooth her nerves. What did she have to be nervous about anyway? She'd made no plans for how the night would really go. She wanted to talk more with Sybil, find out why she had said the others betrayed her, ask her questions she'd been too shy to ask before. That was one possible way for the evening to develop.

Then there was Daniel. She couldn't just keep him in the background. She wanted him to see her, that was all. If he saw her and turned away to his group of friends, that was enough. But she couldn't imagine him doing that. He wouldn't ignore her tonight, especially if she was confident. *Confidence*, she said to herself with total conviction (aware that she was creating one of those teenage aphorisms that bloom frequently and are just as frequently forgotten) *means believing you've become who you're meant to be.* Sybil's sister Candance opened the door to her. She was early; only a few people had arrived. Sybil's sister and her guy friends had already gotten drunk watching the early baseball game and then they'd sobered up and now they were drinking again. They'd set up the ping pong table on the patio and music was playing on a cordless stereo on one of the cast iron patio chairs.

"Wow, you look like you're about to burst out of there," Sybil said, hugging Jessica and giving her a peck on the cheek. She even had to take a cocktail napkin and wipe Jessica's cheek where her dark lipstick had left a splotch. "I've never told you but you're a stunning sixteen-year-old woman."

"Gosh, gee," Jessica said.

"How about a drink?" They drank martinis while the older guys goofed off, peripherally aware of female attention. The television was on in the family room, the next room over, the noise of guns came from some movie Jessica didn't recognize.

More people arrived. They had started to let themselves in and Booth McGinty the center on the boy's football team, hefted a keg onto his shoulder. He had to transport the keg around the house through the gate and on his way he performed a few tricks to show off his biceps.

"Hi, Jess," everyone said when they passed. They were all so friendly and on good terms.

Soon there were lightning bugs under the magnolia and linden trees and the Frasier fir trees along the property line faded into blue shadows like they were etched in charcoal. Jessica stood by the ping pong table watching the boys who were drinking. Then she wandered through the airconditioned house. Sybil's house seemed like a hotel because of the lack of clutter, the minimalist design of the kitchen, and dining room with its high ceilings and huge chandelier.

"Hey Jessica," someone said. It was Fiona. She was wearing a Ramone's T-shirt and frayed bell-bottom jeans and no shoes at all. The bottoms of her feet were pink while the tops were gray like a flounder. She carried a clove cigarette and her teeth were stained between bright fuchsia lipstick. "This is Edouard." She introduced Jessica to her boyfriend, although they'd already met twice if not more times by then. They shook hands formally. "Fancy a walk," Fiona said, smiling carelessly and holding onto Jessica as if for support. "I can only stay for half an hour." She allowed Edouard to light her cigarette on the patio away from the ping pong table and all the commotion.

"Big plans?" Jessica said.

Fiona winked. "Not hardly. What's new with you?"

Jessica recounted her summer, the days hanging around, Maggie, Neva, Sybil. Edouard went to find a beer and then Daniel and Andy Mast came over.

"Hey, Jessica. Hey, Fiona. Hey, Fiona, to what do we owe this honor?" It was Andy speaking. Daniel's eyes were wet and shy and he pawed the ground with his shoe.

Fiona laughed. "I know. I never see you anymore. I'm working, you're working. Someone has to make money to buy the beer."

"Sybil's parents," Andy said. "They buy the beer."

"Be nice," Fiona said. "No hurt feelings tonight."

"Well, speaking of beer, can I get you one?"

"Edouard's got it. Get one for Jessica. She's going on a bender."

"Will do," Daniel said. It was the first time he'd said anything. "Be right back."

"Later, gator."

When the boys had gone, Fiona turned to Jessica and said, "Daniel was so much funnier when he was going out with Sybil."

Jessica's mouth went sour. "He went out with Sybil?"

"Only first semester. Last year." Fiona held her cigarette away from her mouth. "He was like her little slave. I'm glad they're not together anymore. It was weird. Like a fling. I bet no one remembers."

Jessica felt her sympathy welling up. "I've got a major crush on him."

"Jessica!" Fiona smiled. She didn't look all that surprised, and she made no effort to lower her voice or act confidential. "From what I hear, him and Neva are on the outs."

"I heard that too," Jessica said, maybe too eagerly.

"Be careful who you listen to," Fiona said. The boys were coming back. "Not all little birdies can be trusted."

The boys were almost in earshot now. "I missed you so much," Jessica said.

"I miss you too," Fiona said. "Edouard. Over here."

"I know," he said. "I'm just watching these amateurs play beer pong."

"Don't go bragging like you're an expert."

"Here you are," Daniel said, handing Jessica a red cup foaming at the top. "Spoils of war," he said.

"Can I tell you a secret?" Jessica said, lowering her voice. "I don't like the taste of beer."

"That's un-American," Daniel said. "Are you a commie?"

"I am," Edouard said. "And I'm saying it loud and proud."

41

"Everyone knows that already, dummy," Fiona said.

"How so?"

"I think the Karl Marx bumper sticker gives it away."

"Do you really think most Americans know who Karl Marx is from his face?" Edouard said. "They probably think he's Ulysses S. Grant."

"Who the fuck is that?" Fiona said.

"Ha ha."

"Communism's a failure," Daniel said.

"No," Edouard shook his head. "You're just jaded."

"He says you're jaded," Jessica said.

"He's just mad he's drinking Natty Ice. He's missing the Heineken or whatever they drink where he's from." Daniel turned red as his voice got louder. "I'm up next," he said, tilting his chin toward the ping pong table. "You can cheer me on." Jessica pivoted to face him. "I can't stand that prick Edouard," he whispered in a stale breath right by her ear.

Jessica smiled instead of answering and went to find Sybil. She was a hard one to find. She wasn't by the pool or the patio. She wasn't in the kitchen. Jessica came back outside just as Sybil was coming in. "Hello there."

"Why, hello."

They walked inside together and stopped in the kitchen and Jessica was out of breath, her breathing was too short. She wasn't holding her beer cup anymore. She must have set it down by the pool so she could walk through the crowd better.

"Does anyone ever fall into the water at these parties?"

"Hasn't happened yet. Cross our fingers. I'm not worried though. There's plenty of able-bodied swimmers to fish them out. Most of these girls had *private* lessons at their hoity-toity country club."

Jessica winced—she, too, had had swim lessons at a country club, not here though and they hadn't been private lessons.

"Do a shot with me," Sybil said.

"Did I hear shot?" one of the older college guys said, strolling by the kitchen counter.

"Make it three," another college guy said. "Wild Turkey."

"No," Sybil said. "But tequila's OK."

"Listen to little sister. Tequila. OK. Fine. Whatever."

"What's the occasion?" Jessica asked.

"Getting drunk," Sybil said. "And I can tell you're sober."

"OK, but Sybil, wait. I need to ask you about Daniel."

"Your crush," Sybil said.

"I admitted that all to you before I knew," Jessica said. She spoke with a special emphasis that had no impact at all on her friend. Sybil's face was blank, but Jessica couldn't tell if she was intentionally drawing on that blankness the way an actress summons a contrived emotion or if she really didn't understand what Jessica was talking about. "About you and Daniel," Jessica said. She had finally gotten her breath back.

"Salúd!" the college guy said.

They drank. The liquor burned and Jessica coughed involuntarily. Then she gagged.

"It doesn't agree with her," the other college guy said. "Let me make up for it. I'll make you a whiskey sour. Girls love them. I'm a bartender, you know."

"Just... please don't sleep with him," Sybil said in a low voice. Her forehead was wrinkled and her lips trembled.

"I wasn't going to."

Sybil's eyes were almost frightened. She had become tender or at least vulnerable, her face contorted and weirdly beautiful. She held onto Jessica's wrist. Jessica's hand was still holding the shot glass.

"I should've cut some limes," the college guy said. "Sorry. That's kind of a necessary step with tequila shots. But Sybil you drank that thing like mother's milk."

"Please don't," Sybil said. It almost sounded like she was pleading.

Right then something very strange happened to Jessica. The transformation she had felt inside herself that had started while she was getting ready for the party now reached its peak. The tequila she drank flowed out through her chest like tentacles, its warmth soothing her body, only her body now felt like it was totally another body, like if she looked in a mirror she would see the change. A thrill of fear mingled with her glowing stupor.

"Please," Sybil said.

"I won't," Jessica said. But she knew even before saying it that she was lying. She was lying to Sybil, and she'd continue to lie to her. Daniel was the only thing she wanted.

VI.

He wasn't playing beer pong anymore. Jessica searched the crowd along the ping pong table, carrying her new untasted unnecessary drink. Then she went into the yard into the deep grass beside the long flowerbed. She wasn't nervous anymore, and she wasn't in a hurry. In hindsight she must have been deluded. She had cleared her brain of all thoughts so she could focus on Daniel. In the moment, this was a perfectly rational act. She moved and made decisions with a false sense of calm or maybe it was a real calm, a soporific, mind-numbing calm, like an agitated person tidying up before committing an irrevocable action. That was how she thought about it later. In the moment, however, she believed she was the farthest she could be from being agitated. Just the opposite: she could see that everyone around her was getting drunk and acting stupid. She saw them—the guys playing beer pong, the inevitable knucklehead splashing in the pool. She saw everything through the lens of false calm. To be so calm was almost like being sober. And yet she was cognizant enough to know she wasn't sober. Knowing that, having that awareness, proved she couldn't have been too drunk. Her point of view was paradoxically clear. But she was too calm to probe these paradoxes. And she'd made up her mind.

She poured her too-sweet smelling drink into a clump of lilies of the valley. She wondered without really caring if the alcohol would hurt the plants. The amber liquid stayed on the leaves like an unnatural sap or like the plants were bleeding. The garden was the calmest spot around her yet evidence of the party had found its way here as well. There were discarded cups in the garden and one broken ping pong ball like a bird's egg under the lowest leaves of a hydrangea. A few groups had broken off from the crowd and gathered in the corners of Sybil's yard by the fir trees and the high wooden fence. Someone grabbed her and held onto her arm. It was Maggie. Alex came three steps behind, and there was Daniel—it was as though she had summoned him. Everything was unfolding in a way she'd predicted. Maggie didn't let go of her arm.

"They're smoking pot over there," she said, meaning one of the groups by the fence.

"Let's just say hi," Alex said.

"You can. I promised my dad I wouldn't."

"What is he going to give you a urine test?"

"Fuck off," Maggie said. "You're always a dick when you smoke. Get me another beer. Do you want a beer, Jessica? What are you having? I saw you flirting with Candace's college friends. You better watch out, Alex— there're elder men here. Older men. Older men are so much more mature. They can smoke without being dicks about it."

"OK. OK. Chill out, will you." Alex went off to the keg.

"Somebody likes you," Maggie whispered. Jessica tried to pull away from Maggie's hand. Daniel had stepped away from them and was eyeing the garden exactly like Jessica had done a moment before.

"I know," Jessica said. "Roger..."

"Nope," Maggie said smiling. "You won't guess."

"What are you whispering about?" Daniel said.

"Girl stuff, Daniel. You wouldn't understand."

"You mean like tampons and stuff?"

"You're just as bad as Alex. Only worse," Maggie said.

"Man," Daniel said. "You read me like a book."

"And you didn't even smoke."

"How do you know?" Daniel glanced at Jessica and sort of smiled. Then Alex came back and handed them both cups of beer and Maggie went, "Darn. I should've given you my old cup. It's a waste."

"Maggie's big into recycling," Alex said. "Ever since that Environmental Science class with Dr. Wong and she learned Styrofoam doesn't decompose. It just stays there. They'll find Styrofoam cups one thousand years from now, evidence of our great civilization."

"Isn't he stoned?" Maggie said to Jessica. "God, I'm so horny right now—but look at him. Weed makes him impotent."

"Really?"

Maggie nodded solemnly. "And beer makes him fart. I'm fighting a losing battle. Hey, Alex," she said. Alex had been talking to Daniel.

"What do you want?"

"Did you bring any condoms?"

"You've got them in your purse."

Maggie frowned.

46

"Girls and their purses. What haven't you got in there?" Alex said.

"I don't know," Maggie said. "But I do carry pepperspray and don't think I won't use it."

"Kinky," Alex said.

"You'd better make up your mind," Maggie said. She went back to the house.

"Anyway, what was I saying," Alex went on to Daniel. "I forget. Let me go check on milady."

"Have fun," Daniel said. "What a slut," he said when Alex had gone. There was only him and Jessica now. "Do you ever feel like you've outgrown everything?" he said.

"Yes," Jessica said. It was the exact feeling she was having. This had to mean something. She had outgrown everything just that very day, the day she learned how she was meant to be.

"I'll tell you one thing," Daniel said in a harder voice that momentarily frightened her. "When I'm in college, I won't be going to high school parties. Don't they have college parties to go to? Sometimes I feel like I'm in a nightmare where everyone I meet I just wish would go away. Am I giving you the creeps?"

"No... no... I feel the same," Jessica said. But she was trembling from the alcohol—she told herself it was the alcohol. She'd definitely gone over the limit tonight.

Daniel looked at her as if he were sizing her up. "Do you just repeat everything everyone says or do you have opinions of your own?"

"I couldn't add much to what you said. I'm surprised because you put my own feelings into words."

Jessica drank her beer for something to do. The warmth in her head made the distance between Daniel and her seem even smaller, very small. Her body was like something held underwater, loosening up, expanding like one of those spongy child's toys that has to soak overnight to achieve its full size. Her hand was on Daniel's side, on his

47

ribs, in an awkward, unfamiliar hold. Sybil had said "Please don't sleep with him." Sybil had known what was going to happen. But Sybil was so undeveloped, like a prepubescent girl. It wasn't Jessica's fault she was shaped like a woman; she was a woman. Neva—she didn't even think about her—not until later. She couldn't do what she was doing if Neva had entered into her thinking right then. Jessica felt the sweat in the palm of her hand against Daniel's shirt and the curve of his chest.

"I feel your heartbeat," she said.

"Pour out that beer," Daniel said.

She did. She poured it on the same clump of lilies of the valley where she had poured her whiskey sour. The foam of the beer fuzzed the leaves. They were walking, not touching, in unison back toward the house. It didn't occur to Jessica to be afraid anymore. She was a virgin, but she felt like she'd done this all before. The locusts, the thick smell of grass, wisps of girls' perfume, the garden where they poured their drinks—she had been here, she had sensed all of it in another time long before. At least she believed she had. Daniel knew his way around the house; Jessica had never been anywhere except the first floor, but now she was going downstairs on carpeted stairs to a basement, and it was like she'd been there too. The basement was large and open. There was a foosball table and a pool table and deep imprints in the rug where the ping pong table had been. A sectional couch framed a large television and off in the corner there was a bar and an additional table and chairs. The couch was occupied by two people under a Georgetown University blanket—it wasn't Maggie, Jessica could tell that right away but she had to pull away her eyes, aware that it was rude to stare. Daniel led her down a short hallway past a closet and an open bathroom. He opened another door and they went inside—a guest room evidently, bigger than Jessica had anticipated from the outside, with a queen size bed, nightstands, and a computer table.

"Is this what you want?" he said.

She nodded. She pressed into him. They kissed. Daniel reached for the zipper of her dress and she helped him. She kicked off her sandals, stepped out of her dress. Her body was expanding again, taut and full and wide in the light from the base of the house. Daniel sat on the bed and let her remove her underclothes. She stood in front of him and closed her eyes as his hands cupped her breasts and her breasts ached as he let them go, falling with their own force. "You're beautiful," he said and flopped backward onto the bed. He undid his fly and pulled out his penis, he needed to work at it with his hands. For all of her forward momentum, she had suddenly stopped still. She'd reached the point where he had to hold her. He would have to guide her the rest of the way. But she wasn't scared. He lay there on the bed like a captive, his eyes trained on her. The moment was lasting too long.

"What do you want me to do?" Jessica said. Right then the moment was over. Daniel's eyes became hard and unfriendly, critical, and she knew exactly what he would say.

"Aren't you going to give me a blowjob?"

"What?"

"A blowjob. You do know what that is, don't you? Or do you need a training manual?"

Jessica stepped back. Goosebumps broke out on her body and the warmth in her head evaporated into a sudden nauseating coldness. She hurried to grab her underwear and her dress and hurried to pull them on, jerking and dancing as if her feet were blistering—the room a blur, Daniel on the bed with his pants open, shadows falling over the corners of the room where the only light had been. Daniel just lay there. She heard him sigh, adjust his pants and roll onto his side. That was how she left him. She hurried out of the room, across the unlit basement and up the stairs. She knew she was going to be sick but she was still in control of when it would be. Her face went from cold to hot. She'd always

49

flushed easily, but now she was burning, her skin crinkling like paper from the heat inside her. The basement door opened and it was light, but only partial light. Sybil stood at the door and it was like peering at an image in a darkroom. Sybil's features were developing in front of Jessica's eyes: she remained black and white before Jessica's eyes were shocked back to the world of color. She was smiling then frowning then her face was full of sympathy but she was still frowning a little too.

"...a heart attack," Sybil was saying, hugging Jessica like a sister. "I've been looking all over for you."

And Jessica hugged Sybil, even after it appeared that others were watching.

Clones

Thomas had the bad luck of always running into people after he'd forgotten about them. Not only that—he ran into doppelgangers, clones, and duplicates of people he'd already known. Just to give an example: Thomas ran into a younger version of his middle school computer teacher, Ms. Breyer, while out for a jog one random afternoon. Now, in middle school, Ms. Breyer was famous for putting all students on Typing Tutor and phoning it in for most of the period. She commandeered the class from her perch on a roly chair where she leafed through old magazines and pretended to complete administrative tasks. But the present-day version of Ms. Breyer was jogging around a school park wearing a sports bra and nylon running shorts. Thomas crossed paths with her and didn't give much thought to this coincidence. By this time in his life, he'd recognized he would continue to see people he once knew metamorphized into unrelated individuals. He'd accepted this as a fact of life which nothing could change. Besides, Thomas hadn't admired his computer teacher, Ms. Breyer. She had been an unpopular teacher, not treated very well at his parochial middle school. When he went into 7th grade, she married a man named Dan McGuire and subsequently hyphenated her last name so that in essence she became a walking pun with the name Breyer-McGuire. Thomas' middle school classmates hadn't been very respectful and part of Ms. Breyer's unpopularity was her somewhat haggish appearance. She had an elongated face like a taffy that had been stretched. Her skin was covered with a double-layer of freckles, her nose was more cartilaginous than usual, and her teeth had an indefinable error that made smiling grotesque. Despite these physical blemishes, the boys in Thomas' class all believed Ms. Breyer was trying to come onto them. As proof they pointed out how Ms. Breyer wore button-up shirts and blouses that revealed whole domes of cleavage, as well as bright satin bras. Whenever she bent down to troubleshoot one of the student's Apple 2GS' she released an aroma of old-fashioned floral perfume and Dentyne gum. A more relevant reason for Ms. Breyer's unpopularity was her inability to control the class or exercise any degree of discipline once things took a bad turn. Her calls to attention were shrill. No one took her seriously. Several times she darted out of the room and returned with the Head of Middle School who, being a soft-spoken, sacerdotal man, chided the class with standard talking points like "I expect better from you" and "One day you will be men and women, community members." Most students settled down after that but the class resented Ms. Breyer for her inability to handle them on her own and a couple of the smart-alecks suggested Ms. Breyer didn't know anything about computers either. She never proved them wrong. Ms. Breyer left the school before Thomas graduated. He heard she took a job at an all girls' school in South Jersey. It didn't surprise Thomas that he would see her again at some point—not the real Ms. Breyer, but an updated one. Some people have highly reproducible faces. In fact, this hadn't even been the first time Thomas had glimpsed a girl with a face like Ms. Breyer's. Back when he was in college, he'd seen yet another Ms. Breyer at a party in Georgetown. Everyone was leaving the house. Thomas was at the door, heading out, when a clone of Ms. Breyer (along with a friend) rang the bell. "Hello!" the young Ms. Breyer lookalike said. Thomas guided them all outside. He explained that the party was dead, they were moving on. The younger Ms. Breyer was disappointed. They walked along together and turned onto Wisconsin but afterward they split up. The younger and prettier Ms. Breyer did not want to accompany them to Rhino where Thomas' friends always ended up. She told Thomas she went to the Cornell School of Hotel Management. She wrote her phone number in pen on Thomas' hand but sweat and contact at the club erased it and when Thomas woke up the next morning he was already trying to figure out what to do about the stranger he'd brought home: a blonde girl with halitosis and a face that was so archetypally *American* like one of those indistinguishable sisters on "The Brady Bunch" that he knew he'd be meeting her too, over and over again, for the rest of his life.

Too Beautiful

Kaylen was without a doubt the most beautiful woman in the world. This was not false pride or hubris or a colossal lack of humility on her part—neither was it delusion or psychosis or "subjective truth." It was a quantifiable reality. Like most of her quantifiable attributes, Kaylen had to grow into this beauty. It was a gradual kind of process. Over time, when she became cognizant of her Mesopotamian fertility goddess features, she adapted; she learned to mitigate and deemphasize her attractiveness in various situations, controlling her looks first with accessories, makeup, and dress, but also through sleight of hand, stagecraft, timing, and gesture, choreographing her movements and using other people and objects as screens behind which she glided as unnoticed as possible. Mostly, she hid in corners and shadowy chiaroscuro. At high school parties this could mean octagonal windows, piano benches, walk-in closets, railroad kitchens—places where she could regroup and avoid the unavoidable gasp of some stranger or acquaintance (or even friend she'd been hiding from for months just to forestall this exact reaction) and the clinging, the small talk, the awestruck worship that inevitably followed. Think how difficult this was: every encounter, every errand, every time she filled up at the gas station, Kaylen was a source of mayhem and fanatical obeisance—think of the craned necks, the shopping carts crashing into pyramids of Nabisco Cheese Nibs, men unaware that their gas tanks were filled, shooting gasoline over the trunks of their cars, women (who weren't immune to Kaylen either) stepping on their children's feet, dropping whatever it was they were holding. In the worst cases, a male could be affected for an entire month. And even when the affected individual believed he had finally recovered, got his emotions under control, had regained belief in a rational universe and a secular god, had rejoined society and become once more a stable "wage-earner," even when the lust and inertia and disappointment had more or less settled and given way to a jaded outlook that baffled only the man's parents and Aunt Ruth or Betsy, even then it was impossible to efface Kaylen's image completely, or forget the circumstances of her astral appearance. Kaylen knew all about her effect on others. For the better part of ten years she had been warding it off. She had the special[1] responsibility of shielding herself from the general public. Every day she went into the world[2] she was performing a public service, but unlike, say, the job of trash collectors or utilities operators or average joes who perform "citizens' arrests" on purse snatchers, Kaylen's public service was completely unappreciated and unnoticed. That was the life of the most beautiful woman on the planet. There was no glory, no renown like Kaylen had pictured for herself back when she believed she would become an inventor for Mattel or an Olympic gymnast—back then, of course, her beauty was in an embryonic state and Kaylen's mother had not yet figured out how to manage and tame her shock of frizzy hair which tended to bushel around her face like the sepals and petals of a coneflower. Nevertheless, even then, there was a marked quality about her which other children sensed and which made adults uncomfortable, though they could not explain why. However, in high school, having passed through the ephemerality of adolescence and the gangliness

---

[1] Special in the sense of unique, not because she exactly enjoyed it.

[2] And this was increasingly rare nowadays.

of pre-puberty, Kaylen, now wearing her hair in an Afro, received the first taste of her beautiful curse. It was after prom when her date succumbed to what the doctors later called a "vagal response" (the result of a smooth muscle tear), but which, in the moment, looked like a combination of fright and rapture when she removed her brassiere at 8205 Seminole Avenue and her prom date took one look and fainted like a downed aspen. Kaylen was much more careful after that. In college, thanks to her infatuation with black lights and the generally bad lighting campus-wide, as well as convenient access to mind-altering drugs, she was able to enjoy at least one or two untroubled romances, always one night stands. In class, she wore enormous tinted glasses so that, even now, her collegiate knowledge returns to her through a patina of topaz. By the end, it was impossible for Kaylen to go anywhere or do anything unless she was incognito and the friends that had glomed to her because of dormitory arrangements began to voice their concern that a) on the one hand, they would rather stare at Kaylen than do anything else, let alone study their notes on Microbiology, yet b) they were taking on a lot of debt to get an education, and whereas c) they were in agreement that Kaylen was beyond beautiful, they also posited that d) having Kaylen around was roughly the same thing as experiencing a series of intense acid-flashbacks, and, finally, e) to put it bluntly, they were jealous of her, as f) no human being should look like that, and g) it was almost an insult to their common humanity for Kaylen to disgrace them simply by existing, but h) hopefully, Kaylen could have a surgical operation to lessen/modify her godly radiance—perhaps fit her with bad teeth or a nose like a proboscis monkey—and give her an opportunity to participate in the world without the massive self-consciousness and fear her condition entailed. Through life, Kaylen could never claim more than one or two best friends. Her only stalwart these days is Beth Moroney from high school; this friendship worked by the mutual understanding that Beth would never actually see Kaylen ever again; they would only talk on the phone—Kaylen's voice being within the realm of normal. That at least was a gift. It allowed her to enjoy the longest of her (not very long) romantic relationships—her relationship with Brent, who she met at a gala luncheon on the river. At this luncheon Kaylen wore a straw hat, sunglasses, and a scarf; she didn't go inside and she wouldn't take anything off. Brent spoke to her with his eyes on her jawline. He was undaunted. Of all her potential boyfriends, Brent was the most intrepid, the most determined to win Kaylen at all costs. On their second date, they went to a now-closed drive-in movie theater, and on the fourth, Brent took her home. In order to avoid her prom night all over again, Kaylen made Brent tie a bandana over his eyes before they made love—even so, his hands felt what his eyes couldn't see, and it was too much for him: he went mildly insane. Over scones and Keurig coffee,[3] Kaylen delineated the entire history of her ruinous beauty, the stigma attached to it, the danger of it, the maladies contingent upon it. Brent remained unfazed—to his credit, he was an actual brave man, not a pretend brave man. And they were together seven months. Seven months, Kaylen tells Beth now! It seemed like a long time, yet it was only seven months, after all. And they worked so hard, around the house, in public—Brent joking that she was his leper lover when others got curious. At night, they had the bandana, until Brent begged for just one look at her elbow— her forearm—her thigh. "Uh oh," Beth had said. She gave Kaylen her rendition of the "slippery slope" argument. It wouldn't be long before he wanted a look at her neck and face, etc. etc. Kaylen had never been a reckless lover.[4] In order to do the public service she had done, keeping herself

---

[3] Kaylen back in her sunglasses and a kerchief tied around her head like some rustic servant in a novel by Ivan Turgenev.

[4] She couldn't afford to be.

from scrambling the brains of total strangers or haunting old men's final hours, she had practiced extraordinary discipline, become a true master of timing and gesture—screens and camouflage. But sex is a difficult activity for camouflage. Brent spoke about marriage—a civil ceremony—a handful of guests—honeymoon in Florence—somewhere where women wore kerchiefs that disguised half their faces—perhaps Romania? Each night, Kaylen revealed a bit more of her body. She tried an exercise Beth recommended: she described her beauty beforehand to prepare Brent, trying to lessen the shock through poetic language. Seven months— until finally, the day (or rather, night) when Brent went too far. "'I have to see you... I have to see you... I have to,'" Kaylen narrated the whole sad story later to Beth who, to be fair, didn't gloat or rub it in Kaylen's face that this was precisely the outcome she had predicted and could have told would happen from day one. This was a year ago now. Nowadays, things are different. Kaylen doesn't go outside much. She has a delivery service for her groceries. "It isn't your fault," Brent's mom had said. "Myocardial infarction runs in our family." Well, Kaylen could bless them at least for the excuses, excuses people make for the unexpected outcomes in life. Brent's family was embarrassed by her. They were prim New Englanders descended from Pilgrims or something. They spoke to her without much eye contact, too ashamed of Brent's demise in bed, eyes bulging and another part of his body bulging as well, unaware even that the woman they were addressing wore a kerchief and topaz-tinted glasses and failed to remove them during the entire memorial service at Trinity Church. When Kaylen left early, they didn't mind.

Errata

Everyone's heard the urban legend about the girl who eats a cracker with cockroach eggs all over it and the eggs get embedded in her lips. A few weeks pass, and her mouth swells up and cockroaches hatch out. Rainey heard the story and for a long time even up till college she believed every word. Once she believed in immaculate conception because her friend Maddie told her this had happened to a friend of her older sister's. Rainey stopped fooling around with her boyfriend Luke in the backseat of his car and for one whole year wore two pairs of underwear just in case the Holy Spirit had any designs on her crotch. Rainey was so muddled she couldn't believe the straight facts about pregnancy until she was nearly a full-grown adult. By that time, Luke was long gone and she'd imperiled her standing with the boys in her hometown. Oh well, who needed them anyway. Rainey felt sorry for girls who fell hard over local boys. Everyone knew the best relationships happened far away from your home, after you'd lived your life. But some townie girls were already thinking of getting married. They'd never leave home or see anything and for Rainey that was so sad. She knew just how they would turn out—stale couples, a passel of children, and something unsavory hanging in the air. Rainey left town the first chance she got and went to an alternative college in the Pacific Northwest. She vowed she was going to try everything she'd been too afraid to try when she was a girl. She hitchhiked, belted Shangri-Las songs in the shower,

and got her legs and eyebrows waxed. She let her hair grow
and then got bangs and stopped being afraid of frottage with
boys. She worked on a kibbutz growing rhubarb and green
leaf lettuce, volunteered to clear trails at a riverside park,
wore men's shirts and stopped shaving her armpits. She
never wanted to have children and looked into the various
options to ensure she would never ovulate. Gradually her
face changed and from her time in the sun the color of her
skin darkened. People said she talked with an accent they
couldn't place. She was attractive enough to be an actress but
there was something slovenly about her self-presentation.
Her hygiene, even at this stage, was poor; she still broke out
in splotches of acne like an adolescent and she chewed her
fingernails down past the whites. She was like a rich girl
masquerading as a bum. Her wardrobe was an amalgamation
of hand-me-downs and Goodwill purchases and she was
overwhelmingly fond of sundresses and tissue-thin skirts
which she wore with unfashionable boots and never any
leggings even in December. In her free-time she read
obscure philosophy and ancient texts that a former
boyfriend (now a junior professor) had recommended and
procured for her while simultaneously marveling at how
much she didn't know. The slapdash education of her
alternative college plus these arcane texts endowed Rainey
with a philosophical framework abstract enough to cover any
problem in her life. Her roommate Meghan privately called
her "L'Enfant Terrible" and, when drunk, talked to her in
that overly loud way used to address babies and elderly
people. For Rainey, each day was an opportunity to prove
that she could overcome any obstacle. She was already more
than content with the turn life had taken. She was
independent, paid her own bills, had a rote job, and could
sleep with anyone she wanted. Already, she had counseled
her brothers and sisters who unluckily were weighted down
with burdens this early in their lives and had already
experienced job loss, childbirth, divorce, and personal

60

failure just on account of being alive. To them, Rainey knew she was a model of success. She only wished they had followed her lead and learned a lot sooner that no one made anything out of themselves until they completely revised the way they lived.

Prelude to a Housewarming

I.

That late summer and into October they spent moving and settling into their new house. It was a four-bedroom ranch house in northeast Albuquerque with an enclosed backyard, a strip of grass, a treehouse, a swing set, and raised flowerbeds choked with the vigorous overgrowth of trumpet vine. The sellers, as was natural, had played up the luxuriousness of the house's amenities and renovated features—the oven had been installed too close to its own wiring, the refrigerator died within a month, the entire circuit breaker wasn't up to code, faulty pipes under the kitchen sink rotted out the bottom cabinet, the sprinkler heads were chipped, splintered and disconnected, and all the grass died that first summer. Still, it was home—the first house the couple had owned—nevermind all the expensive lessons in home repair, the consequences of cheap renovation. They had the walls painted a lighter, brighter shade of off-white. Isaac purchased almost two hundred dollars' worth of gardening tools and went to work on the trumpet vine; he dug out the tough grass, clipped back the rose bushes, planted mint around the alley between houses. Laney hung pictures, replaced some of the hideous light fixtures, and price shopped on the internet for a new bed frame now that Isaac had prevailed upon her to buy a king-size bed.

The couple's children, Ethan and Carley, had quickly adapted to their new home—it was the largest house they'd ever lived in. They finally had their own rooms which were just as quickly overrun with their stuffed animals and Legos, bath-time action figures and cardboard blocks. Carley was not quite old enough to go outside on her own, and Isaac and Laney didn't trust Ethan to supervise her, especially when it came to the treehouse and the rose bushes and the other less obvious dangers of a backyard that wasn't completely visible from inside the house. But Isaac and Laney were loosening up as parents; it was a process that had started with Carley's birth when they were still living in Las Cruces. Carley didn't have the same implacable wail that Ethan had had as an infant—from the first week, she slept a comfortable six hours and was only fussy around eight p.m., needing a thirty-minute car ride around the ghostly streets. One or two weeks after they'd moved, Isaac clicked shut the patio door, waved at Carley, and then led Laney to their bedroom to make love on the mattress on the floor. They could hear the kids outside in a corner of the yard near the treehouse, and afterward, Isaac lay beside his wife and listened to the thrumming, infrastructural sounds of the house, his and Laney's house, waiting for the inevitable piercing scream of his young daughter telling him yet again that Ethan was bothering her—his cue that it was time to get up, get dressed, and be a dad.

II.

They had lived in the house less than eight months when it happened. Laney called Isaac while he was teaching, so he didn't even know right away they had been robbed. Isaac cancelled his remaining classes and drove from the university, passing close to the first apartment they'd lived in when they moved to Albuquerque. Isaac drove recklessly— too fast. He passed cars in both lanes and didn't worry about

63

red lights. Just a year of living in Albuquerque had taught him nothing he could do in a car—short of flipping the vehicle onto a sidewalk—would get him into trouble. He could have driven home on the freeway, but it was more satisfying to drive fast on the two- and three-lane streets, through neighborhoods that had become his first familiar territory.

Every time he moved somewhere new, he was overwhelmed. He didn't know if this was a natural human reaction or if it was specific to him, but his first instinct whenever he moved to a new city had been to turn around and flee. He was instantly intimidated by any new place, the complexity of it, the intricacies and unknowns that surrounded him. This was true for small towns and cities— he'd felt the same way his first night in Las Cruces when he'd gotten off the highway and had the impression that he was driving along the edge of a cliff, a sense of vertigo as the buildings and restaurants and hotels seemed to rise along the road on a crest that obstructed his view. The feeling only lasted a few days. Then, as he built his routine into a new place, the distances shortened. He would no longer depend upon the major roads, and the stores and strip malls would cease to be novelties and become more like guideposts that an actual resident could ignore. The vast unknown place would little by little become home, and surprises would be rarer and rarer and much more pleasant, not ominous at all, like the discovery of a small coffee shop, a breakfast place, a better Mexican restaurant.

Isaac had been thrown into Albuquerque so quickly, simultaneously interviewing and apartment and daycare hunting, that this city had (for the first time) worn off its edges even faster. Laney had grown up in the city and her parents still lived here: that helped. The children loved being so close to their grandparents. They loved their grandparents' spacious backyard, with actual trees, and their little dog, Oscar, who they'd found twelve years ago wandering around the mesa. Albuquerque was expanding. The desert was giving way to new developments, houses with energy-saving designs. On the west side, homes were still very affordable, but all Laney's friends recommended they look east. That was where they'd ended up: on the east side of the city, near an east-west corridor that connected with the highway. They could drive anywhere quickly—in any direction. "And we aren't next door to your parents," Isaac had told Laney. She had frowned, then she'd poked him. "That's better for everyone, don't you think?" she'd said. This was their home too, everyone was happy. Until now.

Laney had sounded wild on the phone—obviously, she was upset, but the tone of her voice scared Isaac. She had told him the story that he was to hear multiple times in the next few days. She had also sounded confused, like the things she was trying to say had slipped out of her mind. Isaac was reminded of a phone call from his elderly grandma who had called his parents' house a few months before she died. He had been in college at the time. He'd answered the phone, and his grandma didn't know who he was—she was panicked, not making sense, breathless, falling back in Spanish. She sounded terrified—even terrified of Isaac. Isaac's parents were away—he was on his way out too— and it was plain luck that he'd picked up the phone in the first place. He'd tried in his limited Spanish to calm her down, but all his grandma kept repeating was, "You tell your mama. Tell your mama."

Laney, on the other hand, had no trouble recognizing Isaac—it was she herself who had become unrecognizable. "What happened is I came home, through the garage as usual," she said. "I got the kids out. I took in my stuff. I didn't even notice right away. Carley was demanding I give her juice—you know how she is. Ethan was yelling for no reason. I'd set down all my stuff, and then I saw the jewelry box on the kitchen table, the ornamental one with the drawers and the key I got at that sidewalk sale in

New York. I thought maybe you'd moved it—I don't know why, I wasn't thinking about someone breaking in... and I was just calling you and walking down the hall to ask if you'd moved the jewelry box when I saw our bedroom and all of my drawers in the dresser were open and the clothes thrown around. The drawers in the nightstand were open, your drawers were open, and that's when I knew someone had come in here and done this. They took all my jewelry from the box, my engagement ring, every ring and necklace you got me for anniversaries, my butterfly necklace, my charm bracelet, my iPad, I don't know what else, what else of yours—I'm sorry. Did you have anything in the top drawer in your dresser?"

"A silver watch, a cross, I don't remember... my passport." Isaac had tried to visualize the arrangement of dress socks and knickknacks he kept in his dresser drawer. He'd heard Laney's breathing and knew she was walking back into their bedroom and into their closet where he had his dresser up against the wall.

"Watch, gone. Cross—I don't see that either. Your passport is still here."

"Did you call the police?"

"Yes. One guy was here already and they're sending in someone from CSI, like the TV show. He told me to make a list right now of everything that's missing. I already started. Can you help me?"

"And Ethan and Carley? What are they up to?"

"They're watching a movie. It hasn't really fazed them. It was the patio door. The patio door was wide open. I mean, it was unlocked. Did you leave it unlocked?"

Isaac didn't like this accusation, but the truth was he hadn't checked the patio door that morning when he left for work. "I don't know. I don't remember. Ethan goes out there all the time and never locks it."

"Ethan's five years old. You have to double-check."

"I'm coming home now. I'm not sticking around. OK? I'll be there in fifteen minutes."

"I just can't get over someone in our house, someone touching our stuff, going in the room where we sleep, where our children sleep. They took movies, too. I don't know which—*Star Wars*. They took a handful of movies. They touched my underwear, my bras, the clothes on the hangers. I just want to take a shower—I feel like I need to wash it off. But I'm too scared to take a shower if you're not here."

"Work on the list if you can. I'll help. Don't worry. I'll be there soon. I love you."

But Laney's list was already pretty thorough. She had written down the big things. Mostly it was her stuff. Isaac still owned an aging HP desktop computer—no one wanted that. Books, journals, even Isaac's old baseball cards—they were all there. He hadn't left credit cards anywhere. He didn't own any jewelry other than the cross and his wedding ring. Clothes, jackets, ties—the burglars had no need for these either. He jotted down some of the movies he could remember while Laney used her work laptop to freeze her iPad.

"It must've just been kids, do you think? Doesn't it look like what a kid would take? Look here, they took the good whiskey your dad got me," Isaac said. "They won't even appreciate it. They also took the cooking vodka. One and the same to them. They were probably high."

Both Isaac and Laney were moving aimlessly around the house, aware that a few hours earlier someone else had been inspecting the same things.

"The cop told me not to touch the door handle," Laney said. "They might be able to get a print, but it's unlikely. The surface is too small."

"So what did they do? Just let themselves in the side gate and test the patio door on the off-chance it wasn't locked. That's some coincidence. And no one even noticed?"

No one had seen anything. Later, the woman across the street told Laney she'd seen a brown van come in the early afternoon and stop at their house, but it looked like their neighbor's cleaning service and it wasn't very suspicious. Their other neighbor Rob came by when the CSI technician arrived. He'd been robbed two months ago—Isaac had forgotten. "They cleaned me out," Rob had said. He'd wanted to give them a friendly warning. According to the woman across the street, who knew Rob better, the criminals had only taken documents and papers from Rob—a much more calculated robbery. This made it seem like two separate incidents.

The female officer from CSI was unable to lift any prints. She told them that wood was the worst for prints, and that they wouldn't have much luck with it. Isaac nodded, and Laney glared at him.

"The drawers have metal handles," she told the officer.

"We can give them a try."

Laney rolled her eyes at Isaac. This officer didn't inspire any of the confidence Laney had expected from TV crime dramas.

"Have you worked on your list?" the officer asked. "Try to make a fair estimate of the value. It's worth checking with your insurance. Do you recall if you have personal property protection?"

"No," Isaac and Laney said.

"In most cases, the insurer only covers a certain amount, and it's very limited. It's worth a try, though—you might be able to claim some of the more expensive items. You said you had an iPad? Well, it doesn't hurt to try. Then another thing you can do is look on Craigslist and at pawn shops and see if any of your jewelry turns up. Do you have a picture of your engagement ring? A picture with you wearing it? It's best if you can see yourself in the picture as well."

"I don't know—not close up—maybe."

"Do you have any photos with you and the ring?"

"I'd have to look."

"And how much would you estimate the ring is worth?"

"We don't know. We never got it appraised," Isaac said. "It was a family ring and..."

"Ballpark it. And look for a picture because it might turn up. It happens."

"OK."

"I'm sorry about this," the officer said, giving Isaac her card.

"Pawn shop!" Laney said as soon as the officer had left, and she had double-locked the front door.

"I know, I know."

"Does she think I'm going to be driving to pawn shops around town? What exactly is their job?"

"There's nothing we can do about it now."

Laney groaned. "I want this whole place cleaned by a professional cleaning service. And I want you to get us an alarm."

Isaac nodded. "You know what? Wasn't there champagne in the refrigerator?"

Laney raised her eyebrows.

"I just figured..." Isaac opened the refrigerator doors. "Well, would you look at that? They took that too."

"Twelve dollars," Laney said sarcastically. "It was the high-end kind."

III.

"Are the bad guys going to come back?" Ethan asked.

69

"No, they aren't." Isaac was sitting on the edge of his son's bed. He had just finished reading from a fairytale book and had put the book away on his son's shelf.

"They took a lot of things," Ethan said.

"I know."

Ethan lay with the covers pulled up to his chin. He looked like he was thinking very hard. "How did the bad guys get into our house?" he asked.

"Through the door that goes to the patio. We must have left it open." Laney had accused Isaac of leaving the door unlocked, and he had accepted that it probably was his fault. He had been the last one to leave. Even worse, he had postponed and pretty much forgotten to call to activate their alarm system.

Ethan received this information calmly, with the same serious, introspective child's face. "They took mommy's ring."

"Yes."

"You'll have to buy her a new ring."

Isaac smiled. "Probably. Some day."

"They took my DVDs too."

"I know. Do you remember which ones?"

"*Lego Star Wars, Star Wars, Elmo*. That's it."

Isaac rested his hand on his son's shoulder. The DVDs seemed to give the burglars away as amateurs—they had just taken a handful at random, not even half of them, to sell quick. What price would they get for Ethan's old toilet training DVD?

"Can you buy me *Lego Star Wars*?" Ethan asked. "I liked that one."

"I'll look into it," Isaac said.

Laney had calmed down and become more philosophical by the time Isaac joined her in bed. "Did you check all the doors?" she asked.

"Yes. I double-checked."

"Could you check again?"

She was still sitting up with her nightlight on. She had closed the window shade in their bedroom although they usually left it and the window open for the cool air. The window faced a bush and was not visible to any neighboring house.

"I guess it could have been worse," Laney said when Isaac returned. "If we were home."

That had happened to a colleague of Isaac's—a Lebanese woman in Brooklyn, who had had a break-in while she was in the shower. The burglars came in through the basement window of her brownstone. They had taken her jewelry too, and her laptop and her husband's papers. She never found out if they were still in the house when she stepped out of the shower. It was a Saturday in February or March. "I was naked as a baby with this going on," she'd said.

"These types of people—I don't think they would have come in if we were at home," Isaac reassured his wife. "They were looking for something easy."

"You think they were kids?"

"Don't you?"

Laney shook her head. "Drug addicts—kids—I hate how they wrecked the place, our home."

"They left in a rush."

"What, did they take my jewelry box and shake it all out on the table? I still can't believe when I came in and saw that box, even then I didn't put two and two together. I thought you'd left it for some reason, what reason I don't know. We were already in here, Carley, Ethan, before I even realized."

Yes, Isaac had definitely left the patio door open on accident. After they had the alarm system activated, they had two false alarms because the spring winds blew open the unlocked patio door. "Careful," Laney's father had warned Isaac. "Three false alarms and the cops charge you."

Isaac tried to be more vigilant, but the alarm made it even easier to forget about locking the doors. He shoved the alarm sign into the rocky ground in front of their house to put all potential criminals on notice. The sign fell over the next day. The earth was baked hard and dry, and he couldn't even push the sign in a single inch. He ended up propping it by the side of the house.

There were a few more suspicious incidents that first year. Cigarette butts in the alley between Rob's house and theirs. A lock on the alley gate was taken off and left open on the wall between houses one weekend when they were out of town. Isaac had thrown away the cigarette butts without comment, figuring they were Rob's, but the open lock was strange and deliberate. It was a lock that opened by key, not code—the sellers had left the old key when they moved in.

"Who would have opened that lock other than the previous owner or one of their kids? She did have kids—a teenager?"

"And what? He comes back to his old house one night and thinks, 'Gee, I'll freak them out and open this up and leave it in plain sight'?"

"Who else would have a key?"

Isaac threw the lock and key away, but the feeling that some stranger had been at their gate taking off the lock was unsettling and kept him from falling asleep.

That summer someone stole the license plate off Laney's car and replaced it with another New Mexico license plate. No one even noticed until Laney's younger sister pointed out that their license plate used to be yellow and now it was turquoise. A cop had to come and record Laney's information and then try to locate whatever vehicle had her old license plate. That same summer, only earlier, Isaac came home after a jog and saw a brown station wagon inching by their house. It stopped and then inched along, crawling down the street. Isaac stood by the kitchen window, drinking water, watching as the car turned into a neighbor's driveway. He thought that was the end—a visiting friend or a relative of one of the neighbors—but there had been something odd about how slow the car had gone, so he remained by the window and leaned forward to see the next move. Just like that, the car backed out and began inching down the street in the opposite direction, pausing at two neighbors' houses. "My God," Isaac said. He squeezed up his eyes (he wasn't wearing his glasses), trying to spot the driver, but the car's windows were too dark—all he could make out was that the driver wore a hooded sweatshirt. He took out his phone and headed to the door, still in his tanktop and shorts from his run, prepared to take a picture of the license plate when the driver suddenly floored it, tires shrieking, and whipped the old car around the corner.

"Goddamn it!" Isaac said. He debated whether or not to tell Laney, but in the end the weird visceral sense he got from the whole episode made him want to share it with her.

"This is supposed to be a good neighborhood," Laney said. "Good schools. I mean, the property tax alone. And now we have criminals just trolling the streets looking for anyone who might've left their door open."

Isaac didn't tell her, but there had been one day in May, during spring intersession at the college, when he'd provided just such a bonanza—driven off and left the front door completely unlocked, though not wide open. There hadn't been any wind or criminal to open the door, and as soon as Isaac got home he had double-locked it of course and pretended that nothing was unusual. They left the hall light on all day now—this was another change since the robbery—because apparently on the day of the break-in, they had turned off all the lights which was a dead giveaway that no one was at home. Laney wouldn't even hear of keeping their blinds partway up like they used to. She even worried that some pervert might be trying to look into the children's windows during their naptime, although this was extremely unlikely given the positioning of the house. Creaky noises at night startled Laney—she sometimes woke Isaac with a clenched hand on his leg or arm. "I heard a noise. Can you check?"

The house's usual nighttime noises sent Isaac into a state of panicked alertness while Laney eased into sleep. It bothered Isaac that their children's rooms were the first bedrooms off the hallway, more accessible to someone coming in from the front door. He had never been much of a fighter and he remembered with some distaste how a good friend of his kept a baseball bat in his bedroom closet just for emergencies. What weapon would he use if it came down to it? His metal desk lamp? The shower rod? His shoes? Or maybe he could stun them with a blow to the head from his unabridged Spanish dictionary and then incapacitate them with his dad's copy of *Anna Karenina* which he had vowed every summer that he was going to read. What good was he if he couldn't defend his own family? Laney of all people had started talking about buying a gun. She said she understood now why people wanted guns.

"But if you shoot someone in your own house, you still get in trouble," Isaac said.

"I think it depends on what they're doing. What if it's self-defense?"

"If they're poking through your underwear, you can't just open fire. You have to give them warning or something."

"It seems pretty fucked up how much leeway you have to give someone who's just broken into your house."

"Maybe you can shoot them in the knee or something—just enough to let them know you're serious."

"You think I have good enough aim for that. I'll tell them, 'Look, I can't guarantee I won't kill you so I'm going to give you three seconds to leave.'"

"I think you ought to have some training before you handle a weapon."

"I'll go to the range."

"You're not being serious? Are you?"

In the end, Laney said no, she wasn't serious, but your views changed after you became a victim. A friend of her father's had disarmed a burglar and put him in a full Nelson and then somehow had taken out his cell phone and called 911 and held the man on the front lawn of his own house until the cops arrived. "No big deal, right? You could do that?" Laney said. When Isaac didn't answer, her breath got short. "See," she said. "That's why we need a gun."

IV.

For a while, Laney kept a running list of crimes that had happened to them since moving to Albuquerque. She included on this list the time a driver without car insurance rammed into Isaac's sedan on Bridge Boulevard, decommissioning his vehicle for ten weeks and causing $14,000 worth of damage over and above their $500 deductible.

"That wasn't really a crime, that was just an idiot," Isaac said.

"What about the punks who robbed us? They were just idiots too."

"Punks?" Isaac said. He was about to make a joke about *Dirty Harry* and this vigilante language, which was a new twist for Laney, but he held back—for him, they were punks too, punk kids. Now that he and Laney had children, he sometimes forgot how much older he'd become. The children grew up, but he and Laney stayed the same, as if the children absorbed their years as well. From age thirty-one to thirty-five, he'd often forget his real age—rarely did someone ask, but when they did he had to pause and make sure he was answering accurately. It wasn't like being a teenager anymore—or a kid for that matter—where your age seems to coexist beside you, always around, like the number on a jersey which you always wear and have no reason to forget. When waiters didn't card Isaac, he got a little upset.

All that summer and into the fall and winter of the next school year, Isaac lived in anticipation of some new crime. He'd considered transferring to a different college, to a different city. Maybe it was time to move back east again. More than once Laney had joked that they'd lived six years in Brooklyn and never once been the victims of a crime. A quarter of that time in Albuquerque and they'd been the victims of at least four; a driver had dented the back of her car in the supermarket parking lot: that was the fourth.

"You guys didn't really know you were moving to the Wild West," said Laney's friend Michaela one night when the kids were asleep. It was Christmas time, December 18th. Isaac had just brought home a tree from 2nd Street. The tree was bare. They were waiting for the branches to fall, but it smelled crisp and homey. Carmen and Michaela were Laney's best friends from high school. Carmen was back for the holidays. Michaela was the only one of the three who had stayed in Albuquerque all this time. She had just been giving her opinion about the robbery. "It's because our mayor is a lame duck now and has pretty much given up. We have less police now than we did eight years ago. When's the last time you ever saw a cop? Think about it. There's no incentive for criminals to stop doing what they're doing."

"You know," Carmen said, "my parents were robbed on Christmas Eve, what, four years ago? Five, because I was in New York, and I came home that year but not on Christmas. They took all the presents right from under the tree—my niece's and nephew's toys. A Nintendo Wii. My dad's phone, because he just left it on the counter like dads do."

76

"That's right, I forgot about that," Laney said. "And didn't they take your dad's iPad too?"

"My brother Hugo put on that app *Where's my phone?* And him and Carlos tracked it to somewhere on San Mateo. They drove over there too—like what were they going to do, confront the guys? Same as you, they locked it, but that doesn't matter. They just reboot the whole thing and sell it."

"And iPads were even more expensive back then," Michaela said.

"My parents lived in that house for thirty years. They still don't have an alarm system. I tell them 'you need an alarm!' These people came into the house while everyone was sleeping—my mom, dad, brother."

"That's really scary," Laney said.

"They work in neighborhoods," Carmen said. "They stake out a neighborhood and work through like three or four houses and then they're gone—like a cycle."

"It certainly seemed that way here. Our neighbor Rob was robbed three months before us, right Isaac?"

"Rob was robbed," Michaela said. "Get it? No, sorry. That's not funny."

"There was this suspicious van apparently. Just lurking around. Our other neighbor Erin saw it by our house the day we were robbed."

"But she didn't call the police?"

"No—"

"Bitch."

"She thought it was the cleaners or an exterminator," Isaac said. But he and Laney had wondered if their neighbor Erin had been a little nonchalant about noticing the van.

"And then Isaac saw this car too—just driving super slow down the street, like scoping it out."

Isaac told Laney's friends about the brown station wagon—he could still feel the tug in his stomach as he recalled the strange feeling the car had given him. Carmen and Michaela listened without interrupting, their faces concerned and sympathetic.

"It's happened, I don't want to say three times, but it's happened more than once to Hugo that he's driven at night and the car behind him doesn't have its headlights on," Carmen said. "Once when he was a teenager, he flashed his brights at some dude in the other lane—not anymore."

"Gangs, right?" Laney said.

"Yeah," Carmen said. "So one of the ways they initiate people is have them drive without headlights, and the first car that flashes them, they follow them wherever and shoot them."

"Didn't that happen to somebody in what's that kind of shady neighborhood by Bel Air Elementary?" Laney asked.

"I heard about that," Isaac said, when the others didn't respond. "Only I thought it was farther east."

"So much violence, man. You can get shot for nothing these days."

"Like that UNM student," Carmen said. "On Central in Nob Hill. That's one of the best areas in the city."

"It wasn't like this when we were in school," Laney said. "Was it?"

"No, it's gotten worse," Michaela said. Then she raised the champagne. "Welcome home."

"That's right," said Carmen. "This is supposed to be a housewarming. Not a funeral."

Later, after Carmen and Michaela had gone and Laney had put dish soap and water in the champagne flutes and they'd thrown out the nearly empty appetizer tray Carmen had brought over and turned off all the lights and locked the doors and pulled the blinds, Isaac and Laney, sweetly tired, both collapsed on their bed, now raised two feet from the ground on the bed frame Laney had ordered almost a year ago. Laney reached for Isaac's hand. They were lying about one arm's length apart. "I feel like it's my fault we moved here," she said. "I convinced you to move to Albuquerque."

"I made the decision, too. We both did."

"It's far away from your family," Laney said. "That's hard."

"Well," Isaac said. "We can always visit. Maybe they can come visit us."

Laney curled closer to him. "They should. Your parents travel much more than mine."

Outside, some neighbors had wood fires, and the temperature was going down into the twenties, and the cold brought out a fresh evergreen smell and a smell like wood and grease and the places where livestock lived. Isaac had opened the bedroom window, looking forward to the freezing air and their large down comforter.

"This is home now," Isaac said. "It's ours."

"We've definitely put our touch on things."

On another night, Isaac would have listed the improvements they'd made—some by choice, others by necessity. But to list them now would have sounded like complaining, like bringing out old grievances. Instead he let the night air and his hazy drunkenness carry him to a place of nostalgia. All the events that had happened to their house had come out that night in conversation with Carmen and Michaela. They had talked about the robbery, the stolen license plate; Isaac had even mentioned—at Laney's prodding—the car accident and the continuing saga with their insurance agency who had now officially recorded Isaac's statement. All through the statement Isaac had said, "Well, I really think... it's been over a year so I don't remember exactly. I'm fairly sure that this is what happened." Then he realized he was hedging and tried to be direct, as he was sure the insurance representative, Yolanda, wanted him to be. But the truth was memories changed, shifted; the way Isaac and Laney remembered the burglary had changed, too. When Laney talked about it with her friends tonight, it was like hearing about a different burglary that had happened in a different house to different people. Or maybe it was because Laney had finally taken ownership over the burglary and familiarized herself with all the important details and contours—the way Isaac familiarized himself with a new city—until the only mystery left was insignificant and all the uneasiness was gone.

"You don't begrudge me?" Laney said. Her voice was heavy; she was close to being asleep. "You won't wake up one day and think, 'Why did I ever leave Brooklyn?'"

"I don't think so," Isaac said. "Anyway, Brooklyn's a long time ago. I mean, I'm always going to miss some things."

"Coffee shops."

"The subway."

"Our landlords."

"The humidity."

"No," Laney said. "I won't miss that."

Outside, a motorcycle droned by, its engine tearing into the darkness, leaving an abrupt vacancy before the night filled in again with its former silence. The neighbors up the hill owned something like four bikes and their teenagers and their friends took them out mostly to ride around the block. Another neighbor had told Laney he was going to write a petition to get speed bumps installed on their street like they had on the adjoining streets. There were a few young families living here, after all.

"I guess I've made a convert out of you," Laney said.

"Something like that."

Laney's body went slack. She'd already pulled her hand away. She adjusted herself one final time before sleep, and Isaac rolled onto his side. The open window felt like a vulnerability now that he was facing it. He thought really he should close it. But the air was so cool and fragrant. He fell asleep with the window open.

The Bear

Before the fire season started, everyone kept watch at night for the young bear that would come down the mountain and sniff the dumpster at the far end of the fire house. The farmers down the road had shot the bear's mother about two weeks earlier. Now the young bear came down, hungry and without its mother, and pawed at the dumpsters and rooted for any trash that had fallen out. "Close and secure the dumpsters at night," the ranger said. "Keep this place clean. Don't leave trash out." They were worried about the mules getting spooked and breaking their legs. The ranger was not a friendly man and he never cracked jokes. He held himself aloof like a bureaucrat and, for some reason, perhaps ranger dress code, seldom wore anything other than khakis, a wide-brimmed hat, and a Forest Service pin. His wife was a firefighter with the crew and everyone called her Sky, and although she was married to the ranger, she didn't ask for special treatment. Sky was dirty blonde and ten years younger than the ranger and they had a daughter, Pearl, who lived in the cabin with them and a stepson who stayed with his mom in Kooskia. The ranger rode around with his daughter and the firefighters loved her and would take her inner-tubing on the river and fishing, too, whenever they could. About four weeks into June, everyone was woken by a rifle shot echoing through the hush. "Sky finally shot the ranger!" they all said. They got up, drowsy, and ambled outside. The lights were on in the ranger's cabin and someone held a lamp on the porch, and there were Sky and Pearl in their nightgowns and the ranger under the white pine tree digging at the ground with his boot. The bear lay like it had been skewered but without blood or shock in its eyes, just as though it were only sleeping. "I got it," the ranger said, triumphant. "Right in the ass." His face looked as if he couldn't find which expression to put on—proud or defensive. The next day he was still telling the story of how he'd heard the son-of-a-bitch snorting around the side of their cabin like a wild boar. He took down his gun and came outside and the bear scurried up the tree still grunting and honking. He aimed and squeezed and out dropped the bear like a ripe apple. Mr. Holloway who did odd jobs for the forest service and was wearing overalls squatted down and pulled back the tarp they'd placed over the animal. "Hell," he said, making like he was about to spit. "It's just a yearling." Then he saw two young firefighters and called them over and took out a bone-handled knife and flipped out the blade. "Cut off the nuts, you know. The Chinese use them in medicine. Say they'll make you strong. Virile." But he was only joking, and he put the knife away. Mr. Holloway patted the firefighters on the shoulders. "He would've never survived without his mama," he said. "Only a matter of time." He narrowed his eyes and watched the ranger telling his story to his deputy and the deputy's Peruvian wife who held an infant daughter in a bright blanket looped around her shoulder. The deputy ranger was nodding and so were the others but the deputy's starkly beautiful wife didn't nod with them; she cooed to her baby and brought her into the shade and waited for her husband who was known for his banter to come back so they could walk to the station together. She was uninterested in seeing the dead bear under the tarp or hearing the story of how the ranger had killed it.

On Roaches and Accidental Impalement

For some time now, longer than I'd care to go into, I've had a fear of stabbing myself. Usually my fear is triggered by scissors—like, I'll be carrying a pair of scissors some small distance from the drawer where the scissors are kept, and I visualize myself tripping on the kitchen rug or on a slick spot on the floor and landing with the scissors in my stomach or chest or something, basically impaling myself and then just lying on the floor bleeding out. It's strange, but I don't frequently have the same horrible premonition of death with kitchen knives, although the two knives that we use for chopping vegetables and whatnot are much longer than any pair of scissors we own, apart from my wife's fabric shears which I never use anyway, and over the last year or so, I've handled the knives way more times than the scissors in the thick of cooking, almost tripping over our children who like to play games and make unreasonable demands for snacks and sippy cup refills right when the meal I'm making requires the utmost concentration and I've got several burners going at once, with water in pots set to boil and vegetables chopped on the cutting board and butter or oil warming in the frying pan and basically all my concentration on the task at hand, overwhelmed by all the necessary steps to completing this meal that my wife would make with her eyes shut in less than half the time. All that's to say, I ought to have an equal fear of knives since I'm often at my wits' end, holding onto one of our long kitchen knives,

83

haphazardly fending off the children crashing into my legs on their toy cars, and orchestrating the progress of dinner which I've said is not my forte. But I don't know—knives never set me on edge the same way. It's mostly to do with scissors and I always envision the same exact series of calamitous actions: holding the scissors in the safe, blade-down position I was taught as an elementary school student, I trip on a loose fold of the 7' by 12' rug or slip on the wood floor, which is always a bit slick after we clean it, even when it isn't wet anymore, and I fall, losing control of where I'm pointing the scissors, ending up impaled on the floor, groaning in agony, aware through the sharp, muscle-tearing pain that this must be something like what an insect feels, only amplified by the sensory input of my considerably more developed nervous system which I'm pretty sure insects don't have. Yet in my eerily foreshadowed picture of self-inflicted disemboweling, I imagine myself in communion with all the ants and millipedes and roaches I've squashed over the years, probably more than 1,000, or at least close to that number if not quite at that nice round figure, and the subsequent crunch of their chitinous shells gives me further reason for believing that the pain through the soft squishy parts of me is much greater and more profound due to the utter lack of chitinous crackling that accompanies my act of stabbing myself. In fact, there is no sound at all, nothing even to muffle when the pair of scissors burrows deep into my belly. Of course, I've considered that insects in the beetle family have something like a soft underbelly as well, though they do everything in their power to shield this weak spot and protect their underbellies—judging by their frantic kicking and spastic rotary jerks whenever you happen to flip them over. Nevertheless, what insects don't seem to understand is that people who squash them for the most part have no interest in exposing their underbellies at all and really just want to trample them hard enough to make sure they are dead or incapacitated so they can sweep them into

84

the garbage or pick them up in a wad of paper and flush them down the toilet. There is something disagreeable to the point of nausea about touching a squashed insect and for most of my life I believed this nausea-inducing feeling had to do altogether with the fact that insects are by nature abhorrent when they come into contact with you. However, since the time that I've begun to fear the possibility of stabbing myself, I've reevaluated this primal disgust and decided that it also has a lot to do with the insects' squashed and mangled state. Things that are inside belong inside, and things that are outside belong outside—that's about it. In the end, basically, insects are a poor gauge to measure the piercing pain that one must feel after falling on a pair of scissors and impaling oneself—it is an agonizing and nerve-wrenching way to go. Probably its very horror is what makes it so suddenly real to me in those moments when I just happen to need the scissors to open some package or container. But what can you do? If you're afraid, you're afraid, and if you predict it enough times, God knows it might come true. I partly believe that all predictions and horrible imaginings contain an element of truth—that's what makes our brains so much more powerful than the brain of a cockroach. Our brain somehow allows us to see what's going to happen and only after it happens or at best in the final moments of happening do we realize how accurately we predicted this event all along in some nonsensical, irrelevant moment that was actually a flash of insight. But the older you get, the more you start to question: why do we need such a brain? How many have regretted its terrible power? Better to be like a cockroach when all's said and done. They were here before us, they'll outlive us, they don't care about us. Their design, in the long run, is infinitely better, less sadistic.

The Secret Agent

The secret agent lived in a small unremarkable house in a residential neighborhood of an obscure American city. For the first year, he portrayed himself as a divorced middle-aged man with two young girls. The girls entered and exited his home at socially appropriate hours under the care of a fetching but exhausted brunette who drove a Prius and sometimes chatted over coffee with the secret agent while waiting for the girls to double back inside the screen door and collect all their belongings. That summer, the secret agent hosted a large housewarming party which wasn't open to any of his new neighbors. It was one of those lively summer parties that hint at a vast and appreciative social network—he even booked a live band.

By year two, for whatever reasons, the secret agent discontinued his alias of divorced father and the girls' visits became less frequent. The fetching brunette pseudo-wife was replaced by a plump Slovakian babysitter. Finally, the girls and babysitter stopped showing up and the secret agent was left on his own, sipping coffee or tea in his immaculately tailored clothing, leading his neighbors to conclude he was the CEO of a company or the type of individual who invents rockets. The secret agent owned a medium-sized RV, a truck, three motorcycles, a dirt bike, and a Toyota Corolla. On the weekends, he washed and worked on his vehicles, swapping them out on his driveway like a valet driver. Over the summer, he and a young friend, a man who could have passed for his son from a first marriage, guided the RV out of the driveway. They spent all of Saturday preparing for what looked like a lengthy road trip. However, the secret agent returned two days later at approximately 2 p.m. He was alone. The remainder of the week, he was visible at his house. On Sunday, he walked a never-before-seen Newfoundland in the company of a slim blonde lady who he had met through a select online dating service. This online dating service—select in that its members were vetted by several first-class security agencies—was just as hit or miss as any other non-select dating service. A month later, the secret agent had dumped the blonde lady and taken up with a redhead about half his age—a disparity which is common among secret agents (see, for example, Cohn, Veronica: *Romance in the CIA*; or Lillian Forsythe: *My Ecuadorian Summer*).

The secret agent thus began to rebrand himself as a ladies' man. He said hello to all his neighbors, was courteous to the old couple on the corner, and always picked up his Newfoundland's prodigious feces from neighbors' lawns. But the secret agent was an unusual neighbor in other regards. For instance, he never checked his mailbox—not once. As the year wore on, he became even more isolationist. He rarely ventured outside except to repair his vehicles or walk his increasingly miserable dog. The only signs of life around the secret agent's house were a fluorescent light in the kitchen and an occasional delivery from an unspecified courier. One week, the secret agent's Newfoundland disappeared, but no one really noticed. This breed of dog was singularly unsuited for the climate of the secret agent's home and had been undergoing a process similar to molting, leaving clumps of its black mane all over the sidewalk where they were blown by the wind and impaled on cactus stalks.

By year three or four, a certain resignation had set in for the secret agent who—like his dog—had likely wondered when someone would relieve him from this scorched desert outpost. The secret agent was so stir-crazy he invited his two pretend children to Halloween and went trick or treating dressed as a pink unicorn, enjoying his old role of devil-may-care father which many neighbors smiled upon.

Nevertheless, the secret agent had already started to experience the malaise and episodic insanity that descend on the minds of agents once they realize they have exhausted their usefulness. He drafted a letter to his agency requesting an immediate transfer. That same evening he broke it off with the redhead. The secret agent's boss notified him via the chain of communication that his concerns had been heard. He was commended for his service and particularly his ability to synthesize large amounts of sensitive material pertaining to XYZ. Thanks to his intelligence gathering, countless lives had been saved, etc., etc. This was, the agent concluded, nothing more than a form letter sent to secret agents after they'd begun to bitch and moan. Even the signature was auto-signed. The secret agent mowed his lawn and poured fertilizer on a lantana bush. He called his actual ex-wife on a secure line. He spent two hours involved in cryptic transactions and—disguised with a Groucho Marx adhesive moustache—made his first trip to the bank in years. By six p.m., he was on a flight to Honduras via Houston, Texas. The following morning, his neighbors were surprised to see four police cruisers as well as a CSI van and an unmarked SUV with tinted windows parked outside the secret agent's door. Regular police officers strolled in and out. The secret agent's friend from the road-trip showed up with a cooler of Michelob Ultras and, observing the pandemonium, effected a speedy retreat. A gentleman with midwestern facial features and large sunglasses stepped up to the door with a pair of keys that apparently unlocked hitherto inaccessible parts of the house. No report was made of this incident. It did not become common knowledge that the secret agent had left until many months later—such were

the low-profile and monkish habits the secret agent had
maintained for the last few months of his stay.

Tempus Fugit

The elliptical machine became her passion. She started the fall of their junior year, right after they first broke up. When she started, she could just reach 30 minutes at one of the lowest settings. After a week, she was going for an hour. She went to Payne Whitney Gymnasium at 3:00 o'clock after Cell Bio. Soon, she added the rowing machine to her workouts. By November, she had lost two sizes—she had an excuse to buy new jeans. She returned a pair she'd bought in the fall and never worn—she'd kept them as a kind of good luck charm for the weight she intended to lose—and the store took them back without any problems. She drank black coffee for breakfast and ate one egg. She increased her protein and decreased her carbohydrates. When she passed her ex-boyfriend at the salad bar in the dining hall, they didn't speak; they just moved in parallel circuits. He moved painfully—his disequilibrium irritated her but she remained unfazed. Her legs were slimmer, her midriff and hips now taut under her hands in the shower. Her ankles declared independence from her calves; she lost the puffiness in her cheeks. She purchased new eyeshadow and blush on the Sephora lady's recommendation. She had her nails French-tipped and seriously worked on her feet and a perennial ingrown toenail on her left foot. Her toes were the one area of her body still swollen with baby fat—they would never change. In spite of that, she painted her toenails hot pink. She was on track to receive an A in Bio. Studying and going to the gym were the twin centers of her new routine. At parties, she was aloof from the group of friends that included her ex-boyfriend. Her roommate Eugenia told her everyone felt awkward because of the strained situation with her ex. She shrugged and said it wasn't her business anymore. Everything was going well. She made new friends who were still intriguing in that new friend way. Her younger friends deferred to her. She caught a freshman named Alex looking at her and she didn't mind. She would go on to sleep with him after a shaving cream dance party at Branford College. The timing seemed right. For the first time in a long time, she felt wanted by others who made the first move. Before he would call himself her boyfriend, her ex-boyfriend had resisted her. His resistance lasted a full semester. In fact, he had had another relationship all during that time when she came to his room and flirted and all but promised him her entire body, in so many words. When they finally got together, she gained ten pounds. Junior year, after three semesters together, he began to irritate her. He grew dependent like a barnacle. They had never really been symbiotic. She'd sensed his need for her early on. After so much resistance, this was an unexpected turn of events that did nothing to enhance his value. They didn't break up in one day or even one week. The process was tedious and long. She broke up with him three times and changed her mind. In September their junior year, they went to the mall. On the bus ride home, he lost one hundred dollars to a hustler playing three card monte. She was furious at him. She was furious at the hustler and the shill who'd egged them on. She'd given him forty of those hundred dollars which he promised to pay back, but it wasn't about the money; it was about him losing in the first place. It was as though in losing the game, he had exposed himself as the type of person who would lose in many aspects of his life—a person who would throw his life into the same rigged system expecting a better outcome out of pride and fear and naivete. After that, she stopped sleeping with him. He was desperate. He turned up at unwanted times. She was starting to make new friends in the event their breakup shattered her original group of friends; also, she didn't want to see him socially anymore. She couldn't quite break up with him. She had invested so much time in him, in them. Actually, she knew quite well she had lost her innocence through him. He had taken it; she had given it freely. She had opened up to him like she'd never done with anyone, and he'd absorbed everything she gave him, remembered all of it. When they fought, he lined up all her faults, reaching back into her private history for motives and justifications that were none of his business. She had started to almost hate him. His searching glance made her insides stiffen. In November, he took a new girlfriend to a party at their friend's house. The new girlfriend was named Claudia and she was tall and had dark hair and a wide, unaffected smile. The old girlfriend was instantly overwhelmed with the old feelings he'd once inspired in her. She couldn't help admitting to Eugenia that her ex-boyfriend's date was too pretty. She was curious about them and what exactly he was up to. The next week she visited him in his room. She undressed and they made love, but like the last few times she felt nothing sensual when his body was working at hers. After, she lay on his bed and he told her everything—how he had met Claudia, what she was like. It was like the reverse of their early relationship when she had told all her secrets to him. She was furious and disappointed in herself for sleeping with him yet again. She felt as though she had acted pathetically and immorally. He wanted to hold her but she couldn't stay. The day after, she was back on the elliptical machine at 3:00. She didn't see a single person she knew at the gym. Around this time Maroon 5 were always on the radio. She listened to their music on repeat as she moved through her workout routine. Something had to change soon and she could feel herself on the cusp of a change. She was closing in on a definitive break with her ex-boyfriend who had made her cry more than anyone in the world—and this was what she wanted. Soon she had brought herself back into the cycle of working out and studying. Her new group of friends had filled the gaps left by the old. She saw her ex-boyfriend ten years later at their reunion. By this time, she felt nothing at all and neither did he. They kissed each other on the cheek and she asked about his wife who had been unable to attend. She wasn't married but was doing fine. She didn't remind him that she had predicted this outcome to their lives more than a decade earlier.

That Perfect Question

It happened around the time I was five or six years old, and
yes I remember it clearly, and no I'm not making it up.
What happened was my bedroom used to be directly across
the hall from the bathroom. I used to beg my parents to
leave the hall light on and they always said it was too bright
to go to sleep if they left the hall light on (because I also slept
with my door open and they figured that the hall light would
keep me awake, which in fact it did), but I'd cry and beg,
and finally they'd say fine, whatever, just to shut me up and
because they were decent parents back then and all through
my early childhood so far as I remember. So the hall light
was on but the bathroom light was off except for this little
globe-shaped African animals nightlight that cast a dim
projection on the side wall of the bathroom and over the
sink. From my bed, I could just make out an oblique angle
into the bathroom. I could see half the toilet and the pipes
under the toilet and a small 4" by 4" patch of red wall
behind the toilet apparatus which the painters had neglected
to fill (the previous owners of the third house out of five that
my parents lived in while raising us had for whatever reason
painted their bathroom red, the color of claret, which struck
my parents as weird and "occult" I heard my dad say one
time since my dad went to Yale and channeled all his poetic
inspiration into conversations about household matters, a
habit which—as soon as I was mature enough to pick up on
it—struck me as somewhat peculiar and embarrassing and

downright depressing when I considered that we, his family, were the only audience for these intellectual "pearls" and that, in the long run, my dad's witticisms only served to distance him still further from the rest of his family who viewed him as a sort of misfit). So anyway, from my bedroom I had a view of the toilet and its pipes and the patch of red wall and a corner of the vanity which my mom had painted turquoise but which looked green like seafoam in the half-light of the African animals nightlight. So that was my view of the bathroom from my bed. So far, so good? I don't think I had any great fascination with the bathroom. I didn't have like some fixation on the crapper or something like that. So far as my parents told me, my toilet training was fairly average for boys. No, I think I started watching the bathroom more out of curiosity or because I was never all the way tired when my parents first put me in bed and did all the pre-agreed-upon bedtime rituals I required: story with dad, story with mom, tuck in with mom, song (Five Green and Speckled Frogs) with dad, kiss and say goodnight with dad, door open, exit parents, etc. After my parents left, I turned over once or twice and usually ended up on my side in the fetal position facing the open door, hoping that my mom or dad might pass down the hall again and blow me a kiss. But since they never passed by again, the only thing I had to look at was the toilet. And that's how my bedtime routine had gone for some time—long enough for me to remember it, even now—until a curious thing happened. Mind you, I was still young, and most of my prepubescent memories have this disassociated quality like I grabbed them out randomly from a memory jar and, had I grabbed another equally diverse handful of memories, I wouldn't be more or less surprised at the images and associated emotions that went with them. I was looking at the bathroom, flitting in and out of sleep, more or less in a relaxed, sleepy frame of mind, when to my surprise I realized there was an odd man sitting on the toilet. He was presumably using the toilet to defecate, though he didn't seem to be in any hurry or to be following any of the familiar protocols which my dad put into practice whenever he sat on the toilet, something he usually did only if he had to pass gas softly and pee at the same time—as I inferred later from my own bathroom habits—or when he tried to toilet train my sister and wanted to recreate the effect of peeing like a woman/girl so as not to confuse her at that susceptible time of her life. This odd man, I was saying, was plainly sitting there on the toilet but after I got a longer look I realized he wasn't even defecating, he was just passing the time like he was on a park bench or a bus stop, kicking his legs somewhat and zoning out. But the most peculiar thing about him wasn't that he was sitting on the toilet with the door open with audacious familiarity as if he were some ridiculous, unemployed uncle. No—the most peculiar thing about him was that he was wearing a red tracksuit jacket and his legs themselves seemed to be covered in muscle-tight red leggings or spandex such as I had seen on WWF wrestlers or downhill skiers. Naturally, the older me knows that this odd stranger who perched on our crapper during my early childhood was wearing nothing more than bike tights and some form of extreme fan college apparel for grownups (Stanford or Louisville or Temple perhaps) but back then, in my inexperienced mind, I believed this little man was almost like a superhero or a diabolical minion because his clothes looked as though they were attached to his body as a second skin would be and I'm not even sure if he was showing any bare thigh at all which meant—at least I figured back then—that he was prepared to pee or defecate out of a small back-flap specially designed for superheroes or devils who don't have time' to remove their clothing to use the bathroom. Now, twenty-five years later, the question that returns most frequently to my adult mind is why didn't this eccentric individual close the door when he was sitting there since he was in full view of a five- or six-year-old boy, and although I have several hypotheses—

and I have hypothesized extensively on the shadowy
motivations of whoever this possibly pedophiliac stranger
might have been—the best, most generous hypothesis is that
the stranger in the cherry-colored tracksuit thought I was
asleep the whole time, as indeed I almost might have been
had I not been startled into an almost paralyzed
consciousness by his very presence. As soon as I spotted
him, I scrunched my eyes closed to just a hair's breadth and
watched him as though there was no way he would notice—
and yes, like I've been saying, he just continued to sit there
for about twenty minutes in meditation or because of some
medical issue until he finally left the bathroom without
flushing or washing his hands. Now, whereas at first this
stranger had paralyzed me with fear as I lay there pretending
to sleep, after he left without even washing his hands or
tidying up the toilet seat, my initial fear turned to outrage.
You see, it was a pet peeve of my mom's that whenever you
used the bathroom, even if you thought you had to pee but
nothing came out, you had to wash your hands. I remember
how we spent a summer day in New Jersey and because the
restroom was too far from the beach I ended up peeing in
the sand dunes in a not very secluded spot. When I came
back, my mom made me wash my hands in the ocean with a
fossilized cake of Holiday Inn soap she had in her purse and
I (justifiably) argued that there was no reason to do this
because the ocean water was dirtier than my hands were
already but my mom insisted and—even more humiliating to
me since I was nearly a teenager by this time—she made a
series of disgusted and sickened faces to let me know how
totally grossed out she was by my peeing and not washing my
hands, not like any pee got on my anyway and if it did urine
was sterile (that was another argument in my favor though I
didn't remember the key truth that *urine is sterile* until after
we'd packed our towels and closed up my dad's cooler that
had contained five Miller Genuine Drafts and headed back
to whatever dump of a hotel we were staying at which was

another of my mom's gripes, though my parents had by that time stopped kissing each other in front of us or really acting at all interested in each other, and to appease my mom's complaints about bedbugs, my dad almost gleefully pulled off all the bedsheets on their queen bed and replaced them with sheets from the top of the closet which my mom said who knows how long they'd sat up there gathering dust along with pillbugs and spiders and centipedes, my mom complaining so much that my dad's goofy smile calcified into a permanent contortion of his jawbones and he announced before dinner at Pizza Hut that he was personally going to "launder" the bedsheets for our mom so she could sleep in the "regal splendor"—yes he said those words—"she was used to." I should mention that my sister and I were deeply, psychologically uncomfortable with our dad's metamorphosis into a jolly washer of hotel bedsheets and after I told my young but already worldly-wise sister that the phrase "regal splendor" was Shakespearean in origin and may have even been blank verse, she told me to "stuff it Doogie" which was her nickname for me back then. So anyway, even tabling for later the fact about *urine being sterile*, which I didn't even remember quickly enough to point out to my mom when she made me wash my hands in an ocean festooned with condoms and condom wrappers and diapers and hypodermic needles and other general filth, I was led to conclude that the real reason my mom was so disgusted and grossed out by my unwashed hands was that I had been touching my privates, something few men can avoid while trying to urinate wearing a swimsuit unless they don't care about peeing on the actual fabric of their suits, which I would never even have contemplated, and so on top of my normal, pre-teen defensiveness over my mom's violent reaction, I felt a secondary, psychologically even more horrible sense of shame and embarrassment and even anguish on account of my own body which I was at that time minutely aware of, right down to the tingling of my clogged pores and the black hairs sprouting up my navel). So, like I was saying, by the second time this stranger in red visited our hall bathroom I wasn't so much scared as irritated and disgusted by him. But of course my first reaction (on the gut level) was still fear. I mean, who expects a stranger to walk into one's house and relieve himself or even worse make a pretense of relieving himself all so he can sit for obnoxiously long sequences of time across from a five-year-old kid's bedroom at bedtime and stare gloomily into the shadows. Another legitimate question I ask myself now, with some annoyance at my timidity back then, is why I never talked to him or screamed both my parents' names since for a long time my sister and I knew that calling our parents' names would get their attention fast as well as cause a scowl to develop around my mom's mouth, showing the slight inkiness of her gums which were stained from on-the-sly smoking of Newport cigarettes she purchased in cartons the size of shoeboxes and stored with the laundry detergent and Woolite and OxiClean on a top shelf of the laundry room—but I never did. Now, I wonder what I would even say if instead of letting out a bloodcurdling scream I attempted one of those ingenuous childhood conversations with this stranger whose face incidentally resembled a cross between Roger Lodge, the host of *Blind Date*, David Dukakis, and Wendy's founder Dave Thomas with a black toupee. I suppose if I had the adult capacities I have now and considering his totally outrageous position on the toilet with his red ensemble, I would have asked him one of those profound and "deep" questions that have been bothering people for generations. Yet the problem remains, when put on the spot it's hard to come up with a really good question. Even as an adult, with all of my adult capabilities, whenever I think theoretically about what question I might have asked this stranger, I find myself stumped and agitated over my own limited and banal questioning abilities. It's much easier to pose theoretical questions from the perspective of my childhood self because taking those parameters into account I could rattle off a dozen questions, for example: *Are you the devil? Are you having trouble? Do you want me to close the door?* One day, walking down the sidewalk on 14th Street on my way to get my glasses repaired, I thought of the perfect question. This question formed in my brain without any effort or announcement and remained floating like one of those streamers that hang from small airplanes over Coney Island—it was what one might call the breakthrough of a lifetime. I held onto my question and marveled that my own imagination, which I know is lacking in many respects and has never been "strong," could produce such a question, this perfect hypothetical question for the stranger who visited our hall bathroom twenty-five years ago and... do you know what? I lost it. In the time it took to walk to the eyeglass shop on 14th Street from whatever location it was where I'd broken through to the perfect question of my entire life, I lost not only the question but the certainty that I would have asked the strange man this question at all if I had one of those chances over again to speak to him and not be afraid of what he would say. I blame my imagination which has not been tested and I also blame my mind which can't hold onto questions or even simple facts (e.g., *urine is sterile*) for too long. In this way, I'm very different from my dad. And I still don't know if I should be happy or heartbroken for that difference. All I know is if I ever think of the perfect question which comes to a person like me only once or at most twice in a lifetime, the perfect question for this intruder and invader of my childhood peace, I will most certainly not forget it the next time.

Wallace Went Home

Anyhow, the real reason I brought Wallace up was she dropped out of school, fell off the face of the earth. I'd gotten the vibe she was extremely family-oriented, like unusually devoted, which I always thought was unusual for someone without any strong religious background. It wasn't like she was Catholic or hard-core snake-taming Baptist or Calvinist or like some obscure David Koreshy-type sect or anything at all. I mean, she was an out-and-out agnostic like me. But family-oriented was just one side of her personality, and it wasn't why she dropped out of school. That was on account of this old high school best friend who she assured me she'd never been involved with sexually. But I'm guessing sex probably would've ruined their friendship because she was head-over-heels devoted to this old childhood friend of hers in this purely childhood idolizing way, some loser named... well, I don't remember his name, let's call him Carl. It doesn't matter. She basically dropped out of school for him—this loser guy, who was also a wannabe artist. She had some painting of his above her bed and she wouldn't remove it even when I asked extra politely since the subject matter was none other than Carl himself in a weird constipated grimace. No, it wasn't above her bed, it was on the side of her bed. It might not have been on the side of her bed, either. It could have been on the wall across from her bed. Who knows? I remember waking up and seeing it countless times while I still wasn't ready to get out of bed so I was too disoriented to remember exactly where it was. Even then, I hated that painting. And Wallace wouldn't talk about the guy who did it at all. Whenever she mentioned him, it was like he was part of the elite. She somehow managed to endow each word she said about this guy with, like, divine splendor, like he was Jesus the Messiah and not some loser high school dropout wannabe artist who was, like, downing his mother's expired painkillers pretending to have a crisis in that clichéd troubled artist way that everyone's pretty much lost interest in since the movie *Basquiat* came out in like 1995. That's what I gleaned from the whole thing. Do I think Wallace should have gone? That was her decision. Her leaving, though devastating for me, was charitable I suppose. I think better of her now that I realize she went to help a friend. It doesn't matter what I think of that friend or if that friend merited her attention or not; that's irrelevant. The point is she put everything on hold and forgot her own ambitions and goals—one of a handful of people in her town to go to college, etc., etc.—and went to help this painter guy get a grip on himself and not fall into an even deeper despair where he might actually try doing harmful drugs. This painting I was talking about on the side of Wallace's room was not extraordinary at all. Technically, I don't think it was even up to snuff with the knockoff Picassos lined up on Greene Street and Mercer. They only manage to knock off the late work anyway when Picasso was basically like *fuck it* and would just paint some cheap looking commercialized purple-faced cubist woman with buck teeth in twenty minutes without changing a brushstroke and then sell it for like $40,000 to some poor sod who wouldn't know the difference. No, this painting by this friend (who Wallace treated as if he were Rembrandt van Rijn) was just a third rate knockoff of Munch's *Scream* starring the artist Carl himself, his distorted oval head going all out of whack à la Munch and blending into this sinister background of forest and trees which Wallace said in one of the few complete sentences she ever said about this guy must have been another *symptom* of his *killer* imagination since where they'd grown up there were hardly any trees at all, just fields of dust plus the occasional cow colony. I'm not belittling her hometown. She could go back there and live if she wanted. I'm not particularly fond of cows. But that was her thing. The way she told it, she grew up in a trailer or a converted trailer in a neighborhood with mostly other trailers and her family was typically broke but hard working and devoted to each other. She didn't have some weird grotesquely obese mother or some philandering father or some molester uncle or live-in relatives of any kind really, not that I know of. Her family was plain, and kind of on the scrawny side from what she told me, and she was scrawnier back then too, from what she remembered. Her dad was like some kind of adhesive salesman or something, not quite door to door salesman-type, more like an office-type salesman who sometimes had to drive their one rusty car around the state of Kansas to various potential clients. I'm foggy on all that. He was also a chronic insomniac and the parent who did all the cooking in the family—which isn't so unusual, lots of fathers cook or are better at cooking than their wives. Anyhow, in addition to his culinary skills, Wallace's dad played the steel guitar fairly well. Wallace didn't remember how that steel guitar made it into their trailer or who they got it from. Sometimes at night, this dad of hers would bake stuff to keep himself occupied since that was another of his quirks: he couldn't stand being idle and he didn't want to disturb anyone's rest or give a Ronnie Milsap/Kenny Rogers soundtrack to anyone's dreams by playing the steel guitar late at night. And during the process of baking or something, he happened upon an old recipe in a hand-me-down cookbook he'd inherited from his mother, who, yes, thought it was odd that her son should be so keen on cooking and baking, but gave him the cookbook anyway because her dad's sister (Wallace's aunt— that is) was a total boozehound and had zero interest in cooking or their mother or anything having to do with the state of Kansas which she hightailed from as soon as she could. Wallace's dad found this recipe for a kind of dough that, when refrigerated, became like the world's best play-doh, retaining just enough stickiness and moisture that it could be handled and squished into balls or whatever you preferred—animals, objects—for an entire day in the high heat of a Kansas summer and still clump together with the consistency of spongy cookie dough but without any oily residue on your hands. It was the perfect play-doh. At first, he made it for his daughters, Wallace being the second youngest. Then he started experimenting with various nontoxic scents such as orange and lemon and strawberry and these were even better. Pretty soon, he was handing them out to kids at the Sunday school which he sent all his girls to for form's sake (and to appease the rednecks) but not because he or any of his family believed any of it. And he started making the rounds, delivering his stock to the local stores and pretty soon the demand was such he had to order plastic jars by the boxload and he was shipping them all over the place using this little 1980s mail machine and carting all the boxes off himself in his beat-up car. It got so he could quit his regular job and then Wallace's mom quit her job too and they brought the boozehound aunt on board and they were working 17-hour-days making the stuff and putting it in the refrigerator since that was a necessary step in the process. It had to be refrigerated at a very precise 40 degrees or something overnight or it would crumble and dry out the same as regular play-doh. So anyway, they became like the town's industry barons. By the time Wallace was in junior high school, they'd moved out of their trailer and into a new pretty large house on a corner off the town square where, like, the two trees in the entire town were located, and Wallace and all her sisters got their own bedrooms and a shared bathroom, and around that time she started discovering a whole new taste palette in terms of food, stuff she'd never even heard of before which some man in white pants and a paper cap would deliver to their actual door: orange roughy, filet mignons, skirt steaks, ice creams with real fruit. And about two years later, as a result of this expanded menu, Wallace noticed her ass had gotten larger. She told me, in one of the only times she ever joked about anything, that the name of her town was Flat Ass on account of everyone being so scrawny and underfed. So, naturally, when she discovered her burgeoning buttocks she was not a little bit ashamed of this visible status symbol, a lipid and/or adipose equivalent of a Rolex or a Tiffany's brand bracelet— which she never went in for, jewelry and that kind of thing, even when she could afford it, maintaining some small-town aversion to anything pompous or showy. In one of the stupidest moves of all time, Wallace's dad sold the rights to his play-doh, which he'd named Smellie-GO☺ with a smiley face on the second O, to some big conglomerate for straight out $1 million dollars, because, to him, one million was the pinnacle of success, and what after paying for the house, and the new car, and a swimming pool, and a rototiller for the grass lawn which was nearly impossible to maintain anyway because of the overpopulating prairie dogs who would just line up and stare at you until you fired a BB gun at them (another expense, for the one boy in Wallace's family, a younger brother: Mick), and the sprinkler system, and a private college education for Wallace's older sister who got into some elite California school... after absorbing all these expenses, plus minor day-to-day costs of living and skyrocketing gas prices, etc., Wallace's dad had whittled his million down to a nub which wouldn't keep through another winter. It's the same story throughout so many small towns: he had to rejoin that adhesive company he hawked for back in the day, only now, out of a lingering respect for the creator of Smellie-GO☺, Wallace's dad gets the title of consultant, and even though he gets paid less (when accounting for inflation) than he did ten years ago, he's also doing less work, since he doesn't have to drive anymore (he sold the car back anyway) and only very rarely flies to Wichita which is like the real nexus of the adhesive operation. So, anyhow, that's what Wallace had to come home to: a deadbeat friend and a dad who's made the whole circuit from rags to riches back to rags. And to cap it all off Smellie-GO 😳 filed Chapter 11—they're ancient history. But as far as Wallace is concerned, the heartbreak's over. I don't think I'd even recognize her. I just hope she made it out OK.

Terminations

The first time he saw the fired principal was at the crosswalk on San Victorino at his son's elementary school. There was a crowd going in both directions and the crossing guard had just blown her whistle and there she was, walking in the opposite direction, her youthful face turned toward him, smiling in his direction but not at him, an obvious recognition passing between them or at least apparent in her glance. The truth was, he recognized her obliquely, a second or so after she recognized him, and even then, he couldn't say that it was really the fired principal at all and not just somebody who looked like her. Her hair, on this occasion, was noticeably blonder than he remembered. The rim of her right ear was studded with earrings. Otherwise, her face was exactly the same. Still, he couldn't quite believe his old principal had shown up and inserted herself into the newer routines of his life. He'd left the school where she'd been principal and begun working at another school and over the course of time pretty much forgotten about her and suddenly here she was without a child to drop off or any obvious purpose for being at his son's school—unless she was interviewing to replace their current principal. Since principals were always replacing each other, and the Public Education Department's secretary designate was always demanding on the record that such-and-such principal be fired, this circumstance wasn't unusual. He drove to work and forgot about it. But then he saw her again, later in the week. She was driving a Nissan Versa with a "Wag More, Bark Less" bumper sticker that corresponded perfectly with what he knew about the fired principal's enthusiastic preference for dogs. Her face was at an angle in the rearview mirror, her silver hair glistening in the glare. When he'd known her, she'd driven a Lexus. The relative downgrade to a Nissan Versa surprised him; however, one explanation was she was driving her husband's or daughter's car. Of course, his surprise at seeing the fired principal in a Nissan Versa was secondary to his overall surprise at seeing her again in the space of three days. This time it was unmistakably her. He could only see her face but he could picture the rest of her body—her compact torso and thick upper legs—squeezed into the front seat of her husband's or daughter's Nissan. He saw her several more times at the intersection of Osuna and 4th Street NW. Usually, she drove a Nissan although sometimes it was hard to tell if it might be another model of car that resembled a Nissan, and really, his own nerves and the rehearsal of how he was going to pose certain questions to the class he was teaching prevented him from accurately identifying the make and model of cars the fired principal drove. One morning, he distinctly saw her on the passenger side of a white truck; he couldn't see the driver. She was twirling a finger through her hair in what looked like the relaxed and carefree manner of a teenager. In her former life as principal, he remembered her twirling her finger through her hair as more of a nervous habit. Other staff commented about her lack of intelligence. It was true she often committed catastrophic misspellings in her emails, e.g. spelling *etiquette* "eddikit" and *outfit* "alfit" and so on. These misspellings were so prominent they distracted from the messages she was trying to convey; thus, she was forced to clarify herself frequently in staff meetings where the librarian and one or two of the more unforgiving educators rolled their eyes and traded disrespectful side-comments. Although she was at least in her fifties by the time he got to know her, with her hair completely gray, the fired principal wore shorter shorts than his own wife. As a result of her attire and her nervous gestures, he'd been able to picture his old principal as a young woman, something he'd never been able to do with anybody else of similar age. He couldn't tell if her hair had been blonde or light brown but he could imagine her dark eyes, thin lips and squat, bottom-heavy body reconfigured in a younger, less freckly woman with the same taste in halter-tops, spaghetti straps, and boy shorts. He drove to work for the last few weeks of the school year on the lookout for the fired principal, passing the pawn shop with its marquee: *Shopping is Cheaper than Therapy* on 4th and Montaño every morning around 8:18 a.m. without glimpsing her, knowing at that point she wouldn't reappear. For better or worse, she'd become part of his routine yet, unlike him, she had no fixed destination. He concluded, finally, that the fired principal had retired from the school system after her unexpected termination and the mornings he saw her were days she had appointments around town. She was no longer counting down minutes or counting them up; she was completely uninhibited— free to twirl her hair whenever she pleased. In other words, the fired principal had smoothed down and worn away the friction between who she was and who she'd been compelled to be. She was laughing at everyone, like him, who hadn't learned her lesson.

Loss

He alone out of a family of hoarders had learned to discard
what he did not need. He didn't know when or how exactly
he'd acquired this ability, only that by the time he was ready
to move out of his family home, he had reduced his
inheritance of childhood memorabilia to ½ its original size,
keeping only the requisite furnishings for his old bedroom as
well as one or two keepsakes such as trophies for sports,
class pictures, pictures of friends, playbills from his one or
two starring roles, curios and paperweights that had fastened
over humid summers to his bookshelves, old bulky
textbooks, and novels worth saving. The rest—including a
cheap stereo, letters from former friends, notebooks,
unnecessary textbooks, unnecessary novels, a machine that
sorted U.S. coins and funneled them into coin wrappers, a
brand-new electronic Rolodex, address books, toys,
blankets, T-shirts, rugby shirts, long socks, boxers with
ruined elastic, postcards and maps of museums and national
parks, wood carvings, piggy banks, jewelry boxes, bookends,
CDs, tapes, magazines, backpacks, knapsacks, drawstring
pouches, fanny packs—he had either thrown away or
donated, taking care to declutter and eliminate the excess
junk from his room whenever the rest of his family was
absent so as not to provoke them too much by his
nonconformity. He had done such a thorough job getting rid
of what he no longer used that he became surprised now and
then whenever he discovered a surviving and more or less

unimportant piece of childhood paraphernalia tucked away in some drawer or shelf or closet corner—a remnant that had escaped his great pruning. He couldn't bear to get rid of these remnants, even if they were worthless. In fact, one day after he'd unearthed a hologram postcard of a grizzly bear that had half-melted to the back of a low shelf, he was reminded of all the other things he'd thrown away and experienced a vague sense of loss, an extraneous and impending sadness, as if he had failed to appreciate a part of his childhood or correctly value its objects. Now that they were gone, he missed the old books he would never read, the yellowing T-shirts he would never wear, the letters and notebooks that contained an earlier version of himself delineated in handwriting he would never duplicate. Return trips to his childhood home now came at important intervals: Thanksgiving, Christmas, summer vacations; they marked the beginnings and ends of things: his children's births, the deaths of relatives. Now, whenever he returned, he slept in the same room bereft of half its belongings, a room like a hollowed-out melon, the old walls enfleshed with posters and pictures of his youth. He could feel a corresponding hollowness inside himself—hollowness with no fixed location—the knowledge of what he had lost. And losing things was so easy to do, especially now, when it had always been easy, when he had mastered the art so young.

Coda

Every year, the famous violinist takes a vacation to this town in Nova Scotia where there is a Scottish music festival and a bed and breakfast she likes. In the early days, she'd wanted to be anonymous—but anonymity isn't something she needs anymore. Her fame spanned a period of four years in the late 1980s back when she really was just a girl. Since then, her reputation has become an item of historical record—those four years a distinct epoch never to be lived again. If anyone remembers her, it's as she was back then, pictured on the cover of her only recording: the high cheekbones and frankly cruel expression of an unknowing yet confident adolescent who, at the time, critics said, clutched at brilliance.

   Her brilliance never materialized. The famous violinist had never been the darling of the most influential critics. To them, she'd always been underdeveloped; something was lacking. If they had to put her deficiencies into words, they were these: she lacked "feeling" and/or "passion." She didn't "feel the music." She didn't play with "passion." It wasn't enough to have technical prowess, the ability to change positions and land the bow on the correct note every time. Above-average violinists could acquire those skills. No, you also had to live in the music, feel its heart and expose its core as if resuscitating a beautifully preserved corpse and revitalizing it through the alchemy of performance. This was what the famous violinist failed to do—she couldn't bring whatever she played to life. For all her proficiency, her playing left audiences cold.

Yet she had required coldness to become as good as she was. When others had been sleeping, she had been working, putting away even the smallest pleasures so she could practice until her body ached. She'd even taken out her violin with a 102 degree fever... just so her father wouldn't be disappointed. She'd woken in a kind of delirium. Her father had been sitting by the bed. She knew it was her father because of his clothes and shoes, but his head wasn't her father's head; it was the head of a rhinoceros. She'd been too scared to point out how frightening he looked or to alert her mother (who was sewing), but her father put an end to her conundrum. "What?" he'd said. "Would you rather I looked like a giraffe? What about an orangutan? Don't concern yourself with me or my head. Let it alone! Get out of bed, don't be lazy, and let's practice." So she got up. As usual, she went to wash while her father readied her music. When she returned, her father had made her bed and laid out her books. Her music stand had been set in its place. On it: Bach's 2nd Concerto. The famous violinist had stood and stretched. Then her father had placed the violin and bow in her hands. "Now. Begin," he had said, sitting down and keeping time with his foot or hoof—she couldn't bear to see. She'd made it through the first page of music when her stand started to hover. It sprouted upward. While she had squinted at the notes on page three, it threatened to bore a hole in the ceiling. Meanwhile, the famous violinist had stood on tiptoes trying to make out her part, and her father had started yelling, "Nevermind the music! Nevermind! Just play, play from in here." Although she hadn't been looking at him—she had been scared of his rhinoceros head—she had known he was whacking himself in the chest with his fist. "Play from here." She couldn't help peeking at him, his head like some chalk-white pachyderm, and then she had started falling, crashing

113

against the stand, which had risen all the way into the sky. She landed in a field of white mushrooms and woke with what she believed was a caul over her face—a washcloth—momentarily joyful at the thought that she was permanently blind and would never play her instrument again.

Her joy was short-lived. The violin was her purpose in life—that was how things were arranged. If it hadn't been the violin, her father would have compelled her to be a genius at something else. But once she progressed, once she started attending the premier schools for music, all other pursuits dropped away. Soon she was going on tour. She went to Europe, Asia. She made that recording which some people still remember. She played with Anatole Kozlov, the Russian pianist, with Eugene Ormandy and the Philadelphia Orchestra. And so it went until at seventeen she was eclipsed. Two younger violinists made their debut and the critics gave them every compliment they'd withheld from her. Maybe those young violinists weren't as technically brilliant but they had "heart." They were also more sociable—they knew how to promote themselves, they were masters at it.

The famous violinist never cared about promoting herself. What was the point of self-promotion when you were already the best? Why else had she practiced so hard, if not to secure her position at the top? But those years at the top hadn't prepared her for the rest of her life. If anything, they had dulled her ability to be happy and made her pessimistic about love. She had never married, never stayed with anyone too long. Men had called her "cold" and "heartless"—the same as the critics. Yet she was never heartless. She was just better at containing her feelings. And few people knew how she actually felt. How it felt during a performance when the house lights dimmed and the floor lights intensified, sliding up her legs, all the time buoyed by her ability to cast aside extraneous feeling. Then the music started, and she was latticed to sound, her body alloyed to the stronger, more pliant material of the music itself: she, the sound-creating center. She could lose her identity in the performance and maybe that was what she'd always wanted... to have no identity, to be anonymous.

The famous violinist's father had died at the pinnacle of her career—a strange, life-shattering event with a significance that overwhelmed her. She was the principal in a Royal Stockholm concert in Korea when her mother called. "Your father is sick," her mother had said. "Can you come?" But the famous violinist could not come—that was impossible, her parents knew that. Her father died two hours before the concert. The famous violinist had taken the call. She had sat in her soundproof room until the guest conductor dropped by to give her some final words of encouragement. Then she had said in a flat, artificial voice: "Sergei, my dad is dead." Sergei had still been standing there as she walked away. She pictured him standing there even after he'd mounted the podium and was guiding the orchestra around her. All she had been able to think about was his dumbfounded expression, as if her father dying had somehow humiliated him and rendered him speechless, which seemed to her afterward as the more natural of their two reactions. His reaction and her anger remained with her during the performance. That had been the first time in her career when she'd struggled with her violin, swiping and pulling her bow in desperation; she'd slipped into the amateur's consciousness of her own muscle movements and the imprecisions of various notes she'd played perfectly well in rehearsal. It hadn't been emotion, it hadn't been emotion at all. The famous violinist hadn't been close to tears or a breakdown or hysteria; she hadn't panicked—she'd just lost her usual concentration. It had been that asinine conductor Sergei who she'd left standing there like a marionette as if he had any reason to be stunned by her decision to perform. His pathetic face had been like an accusation: "This is how a normal person takes this kind of news. You are obviously

some sort of unfeeling freak. *This* is a human reaction."
Nevermind the fact that her own father would have been the
first to clap his hands and say, "Snap out of it! Get on with
your playing and stop wasting time," the way he used to
demand she play the same phrase in the Etudes, over and
over, until the repetition cramped her upper body, and
finally her mother would come in the room and her father
would tell her, "Leave her be. Don't you know not to come
in here when she's playing?" and the famous violinist would
nod and say, "I'm fine, now, Mama. Please." When the
third movement had ended, the audience clapped for much
longer than usual, for a full minute (she thought). She
clasped her flowers and bowed off the stage. "Magnificent,"
the oboist told her. Later, she hadn't been less shocked to
read, *Mendelssohn's familiar concerto still has the power to
astound us as in this recent performance by young violinist
NL. Here, for the first time, it was as if she really felt the
passion of the music; she gave us a performance worthy of
life itself.* Sergei had met her afterward, on her way out. He
had clasped her hand. "I can't let you go like this. Let me
take you to the hotel." But she pulled away. The next
morning, she took a flight to New York via Los Angeles and
the rest of her engagements with Stockholm were
postponed. For one night, she had shown them! It couldn't
last. Even by the next year, she was starting to be forgotten.

Today, the first day of her arrival in this small coastal
town of sheer cliff faces, she takes a bike ride and thinks:
everyone, every person will be forgotten. As a girl, she would
have resented this. She would have rebelled. "Not me," she
would have said. "No one will forget me." The glory of fame
would preserve her like the names of the composers whose
music she called into life. But now she has a different point
of view. There is nothing wrong with being forgotten, she
decides. Blending into the past and the future all at once.
Being forgotten: giving yourself trembling to the unknown.

Acknowledgements

I am grateful to the editors and readers of the following publications in which these stories first appeared:

The Esthetic Apostle, "Parallel Lines" (2018)

The Raw Art Review, "The Wedding" (2019)

Wraparound South, "Turnabout" (2019)

Garfield Lake Review, "Talking My Generation Blues" (2019)

Digging Through the Fat, "Wallace Made Good" appearing as "The Hive" (2018)

Cagibi, "Prelude to a Housewarming" (2019)

ELM, "Tempus Fugit" (2019)

Litro Online, "Wallace Went Home" (2019)

Typishly, "Too Beautiful" (2017)

To early readers and editors, I couldn't have done this without you. I'd especially like to thank Gessy Alvarez of *Digging Through the Fat* and Samuel Griffin of *The Esthetic Apostle* for picking my stories out of the slush pile and encouraging me to keep on keeping on. Thank you to Henry Stanton and the team at Uncollected Press for believing in my manuscript and for their straightforward approach. Danny Kucer, thank you for driving me across the country so I could attend NSMU and for your hilarious recollections of our HS years (some of which made it into this book). Liz and Gavin Harkins: you rock. Barry Pearce, Emily Haymans, Alex Hallwyler and Gautam Emani, I appreciate your feedback on drafts of these stories. My Martinez cousins: keep being awesome. Thank you Amy Dupcak and Elizabeth Cook for thoughtful editing and proofreading. The Weber family: for love and support. My parents, Anita and Theodore Clattenburg, Jr.: you opened up a world of imagination and I'll never forget it. Thank you, Amanda, for putting up with me, 12 years and counting! Last, a shout out to the Cyberscribes Writing Group in Albuquerque, New Mexico who are always positive, friendly, and enthusiastic about everyone's work. And to everyone who is a teacher, you're not unnoticed.

Bio

Will Clattenburg has published stories and nonfiction in
Litro, The Raw Art Review, Toho Journal, Cagibi,
NUNUM, New Mexico Magazine, and other journals. He
earned an MFA in Creative Writing from New Mexico State
University, and graduated with a BA in English from Yale.
He lives in Albuquerque, New Mexico.

Manufactured by Amazon.ca
Bolton, ON

24500179R00074